TOLL BRIDGE

Toll Bridge

The Risk of Belief

WARDAN STANLO
WISCHOWSKI

WanderingSpiritWarrior

When I decided to permanently leave my birth home, the U.S., I had a long list of places I could go. And a short list of filters. But somehow I got my choice down to Cantabria, Spain. A lot of paperwork here and a nudge of fate there and... I ended up on one of the Balearic Islands of Spain instead. I thought I'd hit the life jackpot: beautiful, people-couldn't-really-live-there beaches, green hills with ne'er a dry spell, and sea-stone walls. Damned if I wasn't infatuated with their sea-stone walls. Well, Menorca's still a beautiful island that I'll recommend 'til my dying day. But I couldn't make ends meet. So I made a plan to move to Sweden, by way of increasing my education in Germany. I'm a bad, bitter student and it would be dirty labor for me. But when I got along, I was finally able to make my home... in Norway. Y'know, lots of paperwork and a nudge of fate.

Maybe it was an early seeded fate. In the first house I can remember, before my life became more moves than birthdays, we had an exchange student. He was from Norway. He was tall. He brought us stinky brown goat cheese, a book of Norwegian faery tales, and for each member of the family, a famous Norwegian troll doll. I loved those dolls, especially my big brother's; his was cooler than mine, but I wasn't allowed to switch. I also loved that book of faery tales. I still have a photocopy and I tell some of the stories to kids occasionally. I didn't eat any more of that brown goat cheese than I had to, though. *shudder*

And then I forgot all about Norway.

Ah, sorry. I forgot to mention, our exchange student was sent back early for being a party boy. I don't remember his name. I was only five. I think I remember something like "Bread-ah." Roll the "r." Maybe.

I got out of the U.S.—before I *left*—you know. And I met other people from outside the U.S. including Norway, even. But nothing ever made me think of Norway. Nothing reminded me that those stories that I retold were Norwegian, even *when* I told them. Do you ever get automatic that way about something? Do you ever live some part of your life so automatically that it doesn't feel like a piece of life anymore? Just a pen you're used to? A familiar jacket? Norway was one of those, another mundane part of existence that I used in order to get through my day, never connecting, never smelling that stinky brown cheese, never feeling the first awe for the long-nosed troll laughing, dangerous and oafish all together.

I'll leave it as a choice to you. The automatic (the regular) way to go through life, it's thin. It's watered down and it's enough to get by. But the way where you remember, feel, and believe in your own life... is precariously thick. It's the kind of thing you may choke on and sputter out. The kind of thing that you overdose on. And for more than a few, the kind of thing that kills you. Like I said, I'll leave the choice to you. If you ever make the choice. I don't think I ever did. Just life all happened one way until it happened the other.

Anyway.

Norway. The mottled green saturates the environment there. Stones and earth form a place that seems older than people. I suppose the smarter ones will call me silly, of course the earth is older than people. But it doesn't feel that way in most places of the world. Some places feel new because of shiny buildings and automatic metros. But even when you get past the shiny, take the drive to the outskirts, and find a view of nature that wasn't planted by city workers, it often still doesn't feel very old. Even old landfills and reclaimed strip mines can have jaw-dropping beauty. And your conscious mind can't tell those hills aren't prehistorically old. But your unconscious mind picks up things. You'll never know it until you've seen a place that's truly old. Then you'll realize that there's something different in the vibrations.

In Norway you can see trees that look like they were there before the grandfathers of grandfathers of grandfathers. They have rivers that've carved their rut so good, you couldn't bend them with a case of dynamite and a bull-dozer. But still those trees and rivers are young compared to the great boulders rooted next to them. It looks like those boulders stopped at rest there when mankind was still picking out their fleas on another continent. And the character, the radiating under-voice of those trees or that river, cut deep, deep in its ravine, makes bold bragging claims that this was there before the myths. This portion of nature wrote the people... before the people wrote the myths.

On top of all this, in the realm of archaeology, there are many ruined stone structures littered on our pretty hurtling space-rock. Ruins that are formed and stacked such that they must have been built by people, in some inscrutable way. But even those things, that *had* to have been made by people, look somehow older than people. They look as if the myths make sense, like when gods and monsters walked on our space-rock, they left behind a few things, just to be head-scratchers.

* * *

I lived in a city in Norway of course, so I wasn't in the middle of this frighteningly old nature all the time. But Norway's cities don't sprawl like American ones. You don't have to go too far to end up in the thick, thick mosses of nowhere. Norwegian children get lost all the time. And they grow up into very clever adults who can never get lost because they always know where they are and what the way is. I got lost in under two minutes the first time I walked into the woods! Someone came and found me right away, but that's how I learned that I'm the sort who needs to stay in the town. Don't feel bad for me, though; when you're helpless, adventure is everywhere!

I was an au pair in Norway. I got two smart-ass kids who never failed to make fun of me because they could go in the woods and I couldn't. That's fine. I never gave them the American candy I brought for them. The parents made fun of me too. Well, atleast everybody had a sense of humor. And of course I went into the woods some, just with groups. But I had to stay very close to other people. I couldn't go to the side to pee behind a tree, not only because I always felt like something in the forest wanted to run up and bite me in the butt, but I could actually get lost just taking too long and coming the wrong way around my privacy-tree. You stop laughing at me.

I was pretty comfortable with my wise-ass kids and their smart aleck parents. I had high hopes for one girl at my part-time job who was looking at me too often. I was starting to think everything had turned out right and that I found the place in the world for me to settle. Ancient old Norway. Mwah!

Yeah, you're right. There was a catch. There has to be a catch when everything seems alright. That's right about the time that politics hit. Some kid went missing. Now I already told you, that was more than normal for Norway. Unfortunately he stayed missing. That happened in Norway too, though much less often. A couple times a year a kid got lost forever. It was such a small number that politics might have never worried about it. But then a politician *publicly* didn't worry about it and that set everything on fire. He had said some flippant remark like, "The boy will come back with a beard and a job." And the raging left of Norway dragged him over the coals for how he could say something so callous to grieving parents.

He didn't really say it to the parents, but never mind that. All of a sudden missing children was a major issue and people acted like it was the government's fault. It's just the kind of over-blown politics I left the U.S. to get away from. More than one political cartoon depicted that politician, or the Norwegian government as a whole, as a fat troll under a bridge gobbling up children, dangling them by their breeches like a bunch of grapes over the bureaucrat-troll's gaping mouth. And they had perfectly trashy captions like, "Where the missing children go."

I would've had a chance to miss all the politics since my Norwegian was pathetic and I was normally blissfully ignorant of what's going on in the world. But this missing kid went missing from my neighborhood. My au pair parents weren't really part of the raging liberal masses, but they were vaguely acquainted with the victim's parents and there was no way they couldn't inform me on the topic. Besides, cities were setting curfews and talking about not letting children out without supervision. I mostly went with my kids everywhere anyway, but now it was like a legal thing. There was a silly notion that *I* was supposed to keep Norwegian children from getting lost in the woods. *cough* *coughcough*

It came close to working. For nearly a year the only problem I had was that sometimes the kids were bratty and didn't listen to me. And I hated that. It made me so furious. It also made me insecure about myself as an adult. Oh, now how I wish I could go back to the days when *that* was my big problem. Things got so much worse than that when the son got lost. He got lost long enough that it was a thing. Not like when a little stinker gets swallowed in a festival crowd and they have to make an announcement over the speakers to reunite the family. My "brother" was lost and missing for hours. Dangerous and traumatic hours. I felt really stupid for not worrying about that first kid it happened to.

And the parents blamed me. It was *my* time with the kids. I was playing with his sister in the living room and he went outside for a while. That's supposed to be allowed. Sorry, I'll avoid too many excuses, but that was supposed to be allowed. I was playing with his sister and he went outside. And I think he was gone a long time without me noticing because his sister and I were having a great time and I didn't think to check for, well, anything. When the parents got home it started to go weird. In Norway, it's nothing for kids to be playing outside. You just call around and find out where they are. But the mom started getting warm-tempered before we actually knew he was missing. It's like she could smell something was truly wrong because of her Norwegian instincts. The dad stayed cool longer, but when he realized that it wasn't just a feeling, that their son was *missing*, he was more livid than the mom. I thought they were going to tear my throat out for blaming me.

Then they sent me out to the woods to look for him. I was dying to get away from their wrath, but me? Into the woods? I couldn't argue because even though that was the craziest idea ever, it was still technically my responsibility. I wanted to ask for my little sister's help so I wouldn't get lost looking for her brother, but I knew they would explode if I even asked. I wanted to tell them they just need to search themselves, but you know, that whole fear of them ripping out my throat.

I searched very, very slowly. I was hoping that someone more competent would come get me and say that they already found the boy and I could come back. I was barely taking steps, looking around all the time, pretending to be searching for the kid, but really just trying to keep my location, and kind of look out for the Big Bad Wolf.

I still have a hard time describing what that early version of the fear was. My memory is affected by what happened since. But I know that way before anything "real" happened, every rustle in a bush made me think that something big wanted to bite me. And the nondescript image in my head was often wolfish, sometimes eight feet tall, always black or a shadowy brown, sometimes behind me, sometimes in front, standing on two legs, or dog style, sometimes talking, sometimes snarling, sometimes hissing like a cat or audibly drooling. It's not like these images took turns; they were all at once. I say "sometimes," but that's because I don't know how to say how it really was in my mind.

Boulders. Boulders watched me too. With eyes. At the same time that some wolf-beast hissed, a giant rock sprouted eyes and watched me pass, eager to crunch my bones and taste my person juices. Before I could turn around and catch those eyes looking at me, it went back to being plain stone, but I knew what was going on. Just plain living stone... waiting for me to get close enough and—GULP!

I did want to find the kid. I really did. Nothing felt worse than thinking that maybe it was really my fault and maybe he was in need of serious help, twisted ankle, hunted by wolves... or all the stupid fantasies I was having. I was just so afraid of being unable to provide that help. So I kept selfishly hoping for rescue myself. It's very distracting when you feel rocks looking at you. You can't really get into your mature, altruistic state of mind.

After over an hour, I was lost anyway. Walking slowly and looking over for what's moving in every little bush wasn't helping anything. My only chance now was to find my brother fast and get him to guide me out. So I really started trying, calling out his name, loudly, desperately.

Fortunately, after almost a year I had learned how to properly pronounce "Aksel."

There was never an answer, though. And he was very hard to see. When I found him he was as white as a spirit. If I believed in ghosts I would've ran away because he looked that much like the dead. He was catatonic too. So he couldn't give me any guidance. It's hard to hitch a catatonic on to piggyback. He wouldn't even stand up for me. I sure didn't have the nerve to try scolding him. I got him on, just picked a direction and walked straight, with him as my backpack. I came out on the road a half an hour away from where our house was. That's not bad for pathetic little me.

His parents were changed people when I brought him home. Suddenly they were understanding and telling me not to worry. They were smiling and confident that their son would start talking again as soon as he had something hot to drink. I was nauseated. I'd rather throw up than sip tea.

* * *

Aksel never talked again that I ever saw. But that wasn't my biggest problem then. Little

could I know that Aksel had gone out with another kid. I wasn't professionally responsible
for Aksel's friend, but still, his mother was very
interested in knowing how I could bring back
Aksel without her son. The police couldn't ask
Aksel what happened because he was silent
as the grave. And they made me feel... Even
when there's no reason to suspect you, the police can be very serious when they ask about a
missing kid. They ask you questions in a way
that makes you feel guilty; you'd convict yourself. You start to wonder if you did something
so wrong that you blocked the memory out
and forgot. Eventually they made me lead them
back to the place I found my au pair brother so
they could investigate more.

Me leading Norwegians through the woods!
I never felt so much pressure in my life. There
was never an exam in college even close. If I got
lost, they would accuse me of hiding something
and call me guilty for sure. It made me dig my
fingernails into my own skin with a kind of hor-
rified, petrified fidgeting. Even when I finally
got them to the right spot it was so hard to recognize and be sure. It's because the image in my

head wasn't really of the place, it was of my little brother's ghastly face. I guess I finally saw
enough of the picture of the woods around his
face. It was by a deep ravine—and a little bit of
bridge.

At the bottom of the ravine was a distinct
blood splatter. I didn't see that before. If I had
seen it before, I might've wondered what it was,
but I wouldn't have guessed that it was Aksel's
friend that he wasn't talking about. You have
to believe that there was nothing I could have
done for Aksel's friend because I need to believe that.

I got questioned by the police for a very
long time. I was starting to wonder if Norwegian
prison culture is like American prison culture. I
wondered how I would speak up for myself in
court. I had many restless fantasies about my
ruined future in Norway.

Fortunately the exceptional trackers of the
state decided that the first set of tracks didn't
include mine. They supposed that the other
boy disappeared, and Aksel sat down, hours before my tracks came along. The police stopped

harassing me and let me go. I was so glad to find out I didn't do it.

I was glad until I realized that I was free to go back to my au pair family with a catatonic brother, who was all my fault. ... ...

The parents were good to me, though. They were truly, unironically good to me. And now I know the meaning of killing with kindness. My skin crawled every day. Every "hello," "good-bye," and heart-warming smile baked my nerves. All I thought about was escape. My host home became prison.

* * *

I finished being an au pair. I got a little apartment to myself. I got a full-time job. And I got a little Norwegian girlfriend. She was fickle. She'd just stop talking to me for no reason for days. The first times I thought she got eaten by the bushes in the forest. Then I realized she didn't like me as much as I liked her. She said she did, but that was hard to believe. I don't know about you, but I don't abruptly stop talking to people I like.

The blood splatters at the ravine became the stuff of local legend. Yes, splatters, plural.

Supposedly there were new splatters all the time. Hard to say if it's true because people stopped going there out of genuine fear. Hunting dogs, feral pigs, wolves, goats—supposedly all these creatures went missing. But the police only went and looked, and blood-tested, if children went missing. And children did go missing. And some of the blood splatters would sometimes be the missing kid's. Now all the Norwegians avoided the woods almost like I did. But maybe once a month some kid would go missing and the new blood splatter in the ravine would match the parents' DNA. It created an atmosphere. People said they could smell the blood in the air. Nonsense, just fantasy born of urban legend. I never believed it, except whenever someone talked about it, I would give a couple sniffs of the air to be sure.

And a cousin of a girlfriend of someone in the police department, or such, would always pass along that the police found some new blood puddle. And that the DNA doesn't match any person because it's a goat or a dog. And the legends grew. The most popular one seemed to be that a witch cult had moved to the town and made sacrifices there whenever they could, especially human sacrifices. Naturally human child sacrifices must be the most appealing to an evil god, right? Some of the people in town even gave *me* the evil eye. All the Norwegian parents turned into helicopter parents (another thing I wanted to get away from in the U.S.). They had to watch their kids directly all the time, and shamed any parent that let their kid walk away for a second. I wanted to tell them they were stupid, but a little voice in my head would say, "What about you and Aksel?" My old au pair parents were still nice to me, though. Killing me kindly. But they were helicopter parents too. Not that they had to bother about it with Aksel. He naturally held onto one of them at all times. He didn't even look fearful. He had been doing it for so long that he made it look natural, as natural as a koala clinging to his tree, in spite of his age.

I could've given up and left Norway at this time. So many people were acting vaguely hostile to me, and the people being nicest to me were hurting me worse. But maybe all the people who acted perfectly normal and went on with their lives, like nothing at all was wrong, were the worst. People I worked with, and people who came in and out shopping, behaved most of the time like all they needed to do was work or shop and that's all. My nerves were well done, blackened and too burnt to even sizzle anymore. I was ready to leave this man-eating forest and its deranged residents pretending that nothing is wrong.

But that's about the time my girlfriend got really nice. She just became more and more affectionate and attentive. I was addicted to it. I couldn't walk away from that. With superstitious people making crosses at me, being over friendly, or just acting natural, aagh! Her affection was an oasis in a desert without sanity. And she was really pretty, I'm telling you.

She started telling me, also, that she was going to inform me what was really making the blood splatters. Normally I would lose my mind at somebody dragging something out like that. I mean, get on with it, why not tell me the first time? But it felt like leaving it hanging made her more eager to come over, and more attentive. So I let it hang.

It should've hung forever.

Finally she was ready to tell me. I guess she felt like she had enough "evidence" to be sure. "Have you ever felt like something in the forest wants to bite you?"

"God, yes."

"Don't take His name in vain."

"Sorry." My girlfriend believed in God and everything else, as I was about to find out.

"Do you ever feel like the forest is watching you?"

"Yes."

"Didn't you ever think there should be some corpses to go with all those..."

She paused because she was too nice to call the only remains of children and dogs "splatters."

"Remains?" I helped her.

"Yes." She lowered her eyes reverently.

"Yes."

"What would take a whole body? The bones, the fur, the clothes?"

"And not leave behind any... scat?" I automatically envisioned a monster eating everything. I despised the witch's coven explanation (even though it made the most sense) and re-fused to acknowledge it in my speculations.

"You just don't see it. No one who has gone has seen it yet. And they won't see it."

"Scat?" Surprised that my merely ornery an-swer was apparently appropriate. "Why not?"

"Because you don't see what you don't look for."

"We should be looking for scat?"

"Stop saying scat! I'm being serious!!" she nipped, "You don't see what you don't look for."

"I see everything in this room and I wasn't looking for it."

That was too much for her. It was callous, I guess, and she was mad. She gathered her things to leave, but she took the trouble to leave me with a final argument. "I was going to try to show you, but... I know you're not like me, but I thought... I could make you see... with logic and reason. Like you like. But you're too arrogant!" Then she huffed, spun so fast her hair flew round, and she marched out the door with a modest, but distinct *slam*.

My girlfriend wore two necklaces. One was

fixed with a crucifix. And the other was fixed with some healing crystal. I knew she believed alot of stuff, but I didn't know she believed *everything*. I was very curious what murderous ghost, banshee, or revenant she believed was consuming these children and goats. ... And I still wanted *her*.

I wanted her to come back. And after days of texting and begging her to come back, and promising to listen openly to anything she cared to share with me... she agreed to come over. The day was extremely cold and dark. The season was getting to the harshest part of the winter. She brought me an extra blanket and premium hot chocolate. She always took very good care of me when she paid any attention to me at all.

After nesting me in my new blanket and preparing the cocoa for me, she started to lay out the contents of her backpack—old faery tale books and Norwegian troll dolls. I loved these things. They are probably my favorite folk art of any country in the world and I love it all: Tibet, Japan, Chile. My love for these definitely helped me not to laugh at the somber way she drew them out and set them up. I was actually kind of charmed and mesmerized. I felt like I was getting part of the culture that's hidden to the tourists because it's almost expired to the natives themselves. Globalization thins the paint of culture, makes it kind of transparent, easy to ignore, and sadly even hard to see when you look for it. I was right about what was coming. I was going to get more old Norwegian culture in that night than should even be possible in this era of internet and instant cartoons.

Runa (that's this beauty's name) began with regular history linking it into the fantastical, monolithic monuments. Those old stone structures that must've been put together with secret and lost technology by ancient pagans, but look like they were built by gods or monsters... in fact were built by monsters. The first appeared on the far away island of Menorca. (My ears perked at the name of that first place I moved to when I left the United States. Suddenly I felt the hand of fate pressing a pointy finger on my shoulders.) Menorca, like much of the old world, had been home to trolls great and small. The smaller ones lived in the natural caves that appear all over the island. The larger ones, too massive to be troubled by the tramontana (north wind), lived with no shelter at all, and no cover, but that of their poorly tanned and strung-together animal skins. (Here I looked at the troll dolls, depicted in poorly kempt clothes, and imagined great trolls, tall like windmills, and ridiculously covered with some chain of ragged animal pieces.)

Trolls have always retreated from the cities of men. One or two travelers would be a very tasty bite to eat (and Christians were said to have the best blood of all, and bones good for bread). But a city of men was too many to handle, so wherever cities planted, trolls were repelled like magnets. Thick forests, like Norway's, and small islands, like Menorca, held trolls for far longer than anywhere else in the world.

And once upon a time...

* * *

There was a prince on the Iberian Peninsula (long before it became Spain and Portugal). He was a wicked prince, greedy and tricky. Eventually the kingdom had had enough and he was banished. There was no direction by land where he was not already despised. So he had no choice but to set out to sea and hope to land somewhere where no one knew him.

It was lucky enough for the wicked little prince that he did not die of exposure. But when he landed on his new island home, he was beside himself with fear to see that the whole place seemed inhabited by trolls of all sizes. He was sure his chances of survival were worse at sea so he decided to hide here until he could make a plan.

However, the prince had caught cold on the seas and had such a fit of sneezing that it gave him away. There was a great big troll who picked up the prince with one hand and was about to bite the prince like you might bite a hard-boiled egg when the prince screamed out, "You're not going to eat me just like that, are you?!"

The troll gave the prince such a squeeze that he was nearly squashed like a hard-boiled egg too. The troll looked hard at the little man and said, "Of course I will eat you like this, you are already fat enough. Why should I not?"

The troll was too dense to get the prince's real meaning.

The prince blurted out, "Well, won't you atleast cook me?! It's a waste of good fat to eat cold!" He was very embarrassed to admit what a fine grease he would make when roasted, but a good trickster wastes no advantages.

Trolls had not learned yet to cook meat. So the clever prince pointed out that they would need a sheep or something to practice on and the troll said that was easily enough done. The prince showed the troll how to make a spit over a fire and turn a sheep. The troll was delighted with the taste and quite ready to try cooking the prince now. The prince seeing his danger quickly exclaimed, "Ah, ah, ah! But there are different techniques for the different animals. I haven't shown you pig or goat!"

So the prince was allowed to live to teach the troll how to cook. And the prince had to be very clever to invent important things to teach like gravies and roasted pumpkins. Truthfully the prince was a foolish cook, but trolls are foolish brutes and so none knew any better. Of course I say "none" because the troll soon invited his friends over for great feasts of cooked meat. The prince became well liked among the trolls and they let him live so they could learn his skills of mankind.

But since the trolls now had cooked meat, they needed tables to eat it on. Simple work is best for a troll. The trolls dug and planted huge, rough stones in the ground, and laid great flat stones across those, far too large for even a group of humans to do. And they did it all to have tables for their cooked feasts. That's why to this day you can see the taula.

It seemed that the prince might have a happy enough life to live out when he tried to give trolls his greatest gift of all, the lesson of how to make wine. To be sure, the trolls enjoyed his badly made wine very much, but trolls do not do things in moderation. The trolls made too much, got very drunk, and had a great roiling brawl at the very first feast with wine. The silly prince was lucky not to be crushed to death under foot, or bottom, or all of the other things that came crashing down on the ground that evening. When the trolls finally became sober, they blamed the poor prince for the whole fight. They started to argue about how to cook the troublesome little man. The prince generously offered to banish himself to spare them another brawl.

The trolls never drank wine again, but cooked meat and stone furniture spread all over the troll world. And no one can say what happened to the wicked prince when he cast out to sea again. Alas, we have no more tales of him!

* * *

This was a part of troll lore I had never heard. I love faery tales. I loved that it included my once home, Menorca. I was eating all the culture up. And when I remembered that I was holding it, I started gulping up my "hot" cocoa and wishing I had spit-roasted meat and gravy to go before it. Runa smiled and rubbed my back for a couple of minutes.

She told me more stories that I *had* heard before. She told me more about Norwegian trolls, how they have more diversity than any other trolls in the world. No tails to nine tails. No noses to double, triple, and septuple noses. Noses even bigger than the head they are worn on. Two-foot high trolls to fifty-foot high trolls, and some maybe taller than that. Rare pretty ones, and smart ones, and ones made of trees or boulders. And the way she told the stories was so clear. I began to see the hairs that grew on their warts. I could tell the way their eyes move when they are angry or suspicious. My quirky little girlfriend was quite the storyteller. But more than that, the tellings had a quality in being shared that can only be achieved... by someone who believes.

It's best to hear about anything from someone who believes. Even if you're like me. Even if you don't believe in a thing. It's best to hear stories that way, but... it's disturbing that someone could think these stories are an explanation for reality. It's disconcerting that someone can be so... unhinged.

Runa finished telling her stories and whatnot. She knitted her brows very hard. She stopped rubbing me and looked down solemnly as if praying. When she looked back up at me, her brows were somehow knit even more and she said...

"The thing that will eat a body whole, the bones and the fur and the clothes, is a troll."

...

"And nothing else in nature," she added, as if I was going to argue something else that eats kids whole.

I laughed out loud.

I didn't mean to, but it happened and I couldn't undo it. I didn't think she was stupid. Sincerely I didn't. It's just the kind of reaction I have, all the time. Maybe it's not the right way to respond when someone tells you, as seriously as they can, that the disappearances and legends and madness and tragedy that have been happening for a whole town for bloody, oppressive months, are from trolls. But it's the only response I had in me. Runa calmly got up and started packing the things back in the bag.

I wasn't sure if she was packing the things back because she was done with them or she was offended. I was still stunned. And I'm not quick in this kind of circumstance. I muttered some kind of explanation that it was a nervous laugh, not laughing at her. I don't know if she understood what I was saying. I'm not sure she heard me. I was in too much of a daze of surprise to make a proper, spirited argument. But packing to leave is exactly what she was doing and exactly what she did.

I mumbled "sorry" as she went out the door, thinking that it would be the seed that would flower into forgiveness so she could come back in a few days after I grovel enough. She kissed me, which was really unnerving because she never kissed me when she was mad. I had a terrible sinking feeling that she was kissing me "goodbye."

* * *

Seasonal affective disorder, or getting depressed in the winter, is a very serious thing for people who live nearer the poles and have much darker winters. It's more serious when your girlfriend has just left you and won't even acknowledge a text. And when nights stretch so long that there is almost no day at all, it becomes a great challenge just to keep yourself going, seemingly forever longer, to see the short day.

On top of that, my town was small enough, and my apartment poor enough, to still have power outages.

When my old host family asked me to

house-sit for them, I was almost desperate to do it. In my damaged state of mind, I didn't properly understand that they wouldn't be there with me. You probably think I don't know what house-sitting means. Of course I understand how house-sitting works, but you don't understand how sensory deprivation works. Your mind isn't completely functional. But even if I would still be alone, it was more logical to stay in their place. Their place was better heated, better lit, and less vulnerable to the power outages that could leave me without even merciful electric friendship.

These were the longest days of my life. Sensory deprivation has another little known effect on you. Obviously being without people and stimulation makes you feel a little crazy, but psychologists have found that sensory deprivation makes you more open to suggestion. You become much easier to hypnotize and much more willing to believe anything anyone tells you... or has told you.

If you haven't guessed from my hints, I may as well explain I was a born-again atheist. I believed in as little as you can possibly believe in.

I didn't believe in gods, ghosts, UFOs, or conspiracy theories. I laughed at people who did and disdained people who sat the fence of not knowing whether to believe or not.

But after a few dark days, living alone, time off work for holidays, no girlfriend and no will to go out with other people... I was a different person. To make matters worse, some unusually bad power outages had been hitting the whole town. Creaks in the black corners of the house, that used to just be sounds of aging wood to me, became the fiddlings of ghosts. Inexplicable moving lights in the sky, that used to just be tricks of aurora borealis, or shooting stars, became UFOs. Even happy little chances that had no reason to cause anyone alarm, became efforts of hidden angels trying to give me a last chance... to come to Jesus. My mind was clouded and crowded with a world of activity that I never believed in.

I needed stimulation. I knew it even then without knowing these psychology tidbits I've picked up since. When the sky won't light up with sunshine, and you have no work to distract you, and you can hardly look other people

in the face, even the fine technology of hu-
mankind (those stupid phones and tablets)
can't seem to save you... there is only one place
to go for stimulation... outside... into the woods.
(I couldn't go to the city. I was afraid of the people. More than I was afraid of the woods.)

In the lightest part of day, which was still
rather dim, I brought a strong flashlight to try
a short walk in the woods. I'd walk to the broken bridge. It was the only destination I ever
learned. It's the longest walk I could take without likely getting lost. Being reminded of my
catatonic brother, and all the missing children
and dogs, and my girlfriend's last time with
me... would certainly be painful. But I wanted
pain anyway. I wanted anything that would
make me feel. (Psychologists have also found
that sensory deprivation makes you seek out
pain.) I believed that the walk would bring me
peace even if it came with pain.

It had a terrible effect on me.

I didn't find the right kind of peace. Absent
of pain, to the contrary, I fell back into a tunnel
of loneliness, thoughts of the empty house, the
ironic darkness of staring at a candle—wishing

that that candle came with someone to talk to, remembering how candles used to be happy, used to be for celebrating, playing, in tiny safe little ways, with the great monster Fire.

But for me... in between feeling alone, I was plagued with feelings of not being alone, but being watched. I swear every time the bushes rustled I could actually hear the growl of the Big Bad Wolf. I would imagine him coming out and asking me where I'm going before he ate me all up. I could see rocks turn to better watch me pass by. I was delirious and I knew I was delirious. I wanted to go back home then, but then again I was afraid to go back home. Getting eaten up in the forest wouldn't be so bad. An interesting end to an interesting life. Did I mention... I was delirious?

But nothing ate me. Nothing even interrupted my progress. The trees were anorexic of foliage in the bleak winter. The snow was thick, but it was well settled and supported my weight. It covered so much too. Only the largest boulders could peek out, those old boulders that looked most like faces. None of the clean white snow made the forest look any younger, though. Even with the rocks covered in faery-white mushroom caps, it all looked so ancient, like the exact same winter had passed over a thousand, thousand times. The white appeared so desperate. If I weren't in dire need to get outside, I would've given up rather than face the ghosts of the snow. But I was getting so lonely that I wanted the ghosts to eat me. Atleast then I would be with other spirits. It wouldn't matter if I were lost in the forest. The forest would be my home.

Delirious.

A hard shiver rocked through my whole body. It had nothing to do with cold. I was suddenly (irrationally?) afraid of death; I was afraid of the bleak white; I was afraid to become a woodland spirit. But still I was afraid that I had no other home to go to.

I put some snow in my mouth and ate it. The painful cold was welcome stimulation. If I stayed out too long I would become numb to the cold. So I bit another handful just to be sure that I really felt the pain. As I crunched through my happy-miserable snack, I surveyed the area, for a good finishing point to my journey. Maybe if I reached somewhere with any old arbitrary meaning, I could stop playing with ideas of dying as a woodland spirit, and just go home and stare at candles.

And after a while I realized I was already staring at something. I don't remember approaching it, the bridge, but I was almost to it... where I found Aksel. My breaths were deep, maybe I had been walking too hard in the snow. But my breaths weren't the quickened deep of struggling in snow, they were the slow deep of thinking too much about the air. Had I been thinking about the air? I was staring at the bridge. I was visualizing it complete, before ruin. I could see it there, like it never fell, held together the old way, by just the lay of stones, before the blessing of steel.

Then, to my consternation, I heard snoring. First I checked to see if I was snoring. Dreaming *would* be the best explanation for what was going on right now, but I felt very disappointed because I wanted to really be in the woods right then. But it was ok, I wasn't asleep. So... maybe I was snoring while I was awake? Maybe I had some new health issue.

But it wasn't coming from me. And it was so loud that it made me feel small, like sleeping at the foot of Grandpa and Grandma's bed when we visited for Christmas. It's the way everything seems so big when YOU are small. And looking around, though my head wasn't clear at all, I was quite sure that I wasn't shrunken, and I wasn't at the foot of a bed. I was standing... on good snow... surrounded by dead-looking trees... nearish the bridge... with just one bush that somehow wasn't covered by any snow.

And just the moment that the first muscles started twitching to walk me closer to this enchanted bridge, I heard something... very big... move... under the bridge. And my muscle twitches swerved me around off-balance, staggering the other direction. The first step only was walking; after that every step was sprinting... as well as you can sprint in the snow. You look like a marionette and you feel like a disabled kid. Sorry to be callous, but it's the best I can describe it.

But curiosity, some ill-borne curiosity, and also becoming utterly exhausted from trying to sprint in the snow, made me stop. Gasp for wind. Find a smell. Some stink that makes you sniff to see if it's real. In the snow? I turned around. I wanted to get a look at *what* made that smell, what made that sound, before I leave. Just a peak and go home with something to think about. It's a good idea. I need something to think about.

I came dangerously close to the ravine. A Norwegian wouldn't have; they know the ground ends before the snow does. I leaned on my toes and stepped forward and forward again. Then that bush shook. I froze and whipped my head at it. Maybe it was a growl I heard, not a snore. Maybe I missed my chance to back away from warning growls because I was fantasizing that it was snoring. What was wrong with me? It rustled again! I stood full facing the bush, in some super erect and rigid posture, arms shot almost straight down and just a little angled from my body, like a nut-cracker doll. Did I hear snoring or growls?! And when I stood my full nutcracker vigilance, but without so much as a wooden sword to swing at that growling bush, with a great silent howl, a Big

Bad Wolf sprang forward and stood tall on hind legs. I gaped cavernously at him, bigger than me, with yellow eyes that seemed like they were moving even when they held still. Like lanterns swinging on a stagecoach.

And then he spoke, in good English! Like he knew I was foreigner! "I wouldn't do that if I were you."

I didn't know what I was really doing, so I didn't have to fake when I stammered, "D-do what?"

His mouth was a little open. He seemed to be salivating. I didn't see any drool dripping down, but his mouth seemed very wet. And his eyes were too alive. "That thing you were about to do," he said.

Now here I stopped and had a reasoning with myself. I didn't try to figure out what it was I was about to do that he was warning me not to do. (Though that could have helped me.) I tried to recognize what was real, which always ought to be the priority, right? I knew that I hadn't been mentally healthy lately. I knew that I could be hallucinating a six-and-a-half-foot-tall wolf talking to me. So I stared very hard at the hairy being in front of me and tried to decide if I was having a hallucination and needed to address that problem, or if I was really talking to a Big Bad Wolf and needed to address that problem. If it's a real wolf, then it should speak Norwegian. But if it's a hallucination, then it should stop when I realize it's a hallucination, right? I'm not sure how hallucinations work and it's so distracting to rationalize when you're being watched by those yellow eyes.

When my heart started beating audibly, it was even more distracting.

Finally, it occurred to me that the safest solution, whichever reality was right, would be to run.

That's what I did. I ran at a tree first because that's something to run around and he's probably faster than me. Maybe I could break a branch off the tree and beat him away while circling the tree! But he didn't follow me. I noticed when I started running that he stood perfectly still. And he called out to me as I ran, "Alright, see you later then, friend!"

Now I had a new dilemma. I didn't want

to be his friend. But I couldn't let him know that. He's a six-and-a-half-foot wolf who jumps out of bushes in the forest. I didn't exactly stop running, but I slowed down and tried to look casual. I twisted back and fake-friendly hollered, "See you!" Then I just kept running like it was normal and I was just running late for work or out for a jog.

The problem is I wasn't running toward home. I had run toward the nearest tree and just kept going past it. I couldn't turn around and get caught by that freak wolf. I'd have to curve around wide, very wide... and get the path right later.

I didn't curve my path correctly. I know you're probably not surprised. I wasn't surprised either; it's just that I needed to be right so badly this time. There was no host family to notice if I came home late. And it was winter now, full snow. And there was a cult of murderous witches in this forest, or a child-eating troll. There was a Big Bad Wolf anyway, or I was having hallucinations. None of these possibilities were safer than any other. I needed to curve the path the right way because I needed not to die, and now I had almost no chance of living.

I looked side to side. I kept running. You're not supposed to run when you're lost in the woods. I read that somewhere, or probably saw it on TV. It wastes energy. And if it's cold and you sweat, your sweat can freeze. But I had to get somewhere fast and the way to get somewhere fast is to run. I just kept running. I kept running when my hips and thighs ached from fatigue. I kept running when my face was suffering from sucking in too much cold air and blowing snot out that was freezing to my own face. I kept running even when I realized that I was probably running more to the wild than to the city. Did I mention delirium?

It was getting dark. And colder. I didn't know how to make a fire out in the wilderland. I don't know if these Norwegian geniuses know how to make fire without any tools and with snow-soaked branches. I couldn't run anymore. But I couldn't stop. That wolf might just be waiting for me to sleep. Maybe that's when he'll eat me so that I can't poke his eye out with a stick. Clever wolf. *shake head*

Besides.

Besides, you can't stop anyway when it's cold like that. You fall asleep and you never wake up. It's called hypothermia. I remembered 10 minutes ago wanting to be a snow ghost. I didn't want to be a ghost anymore. I wanted to live.

I was going to trudge all night to keep myself warm enough until the dawn came again.

I came back to consciousness, kind of collapse-leaned against a tall tree. I had been sleeping somehow. I had snorted a fresh, wind-blown snowflake into my nose and it roused me. Or else I would have died there... sleeping... frozen to a tree trunk. I looked around and saw a light in the distance. I started running in my mind, but in the real world I was too stiff. I could barely move at all. I mummy staggered toward the light. Every time a tree came between me and the light I panicked; I thought the light was just another hallucination and I was going to die alone in the woods, not a content ghost, but a hungry and tortured evil spirit, bound forever, trying to exact revenge from the nobody and nothing whose fault it was that my corpse fell there. But as I shambled on, the light always reappeared. It wasn't a hallucination. Probably. One time when it disappeared I thought it was the wolf that came up between me and the light. But I didn't get eaten. There was no wolf. And in my weakened state I finally got... to the cabin.

I knocked on the door by the glowing window. When I came to, an old lady was opening the door while I was... embarrassingly... well, I had my mouth on the door frame, vacantly gnawing on the wood. Did I mention delirium? But the light lit me up and the warm could be felt by my eyes, the only part of me that wasn't too numb to feel. And the old lady said something, probably, "You poor dear." But probably in Norwegian. And she walked me in. In fact, I think she held me up like I was old and she was young. And she leaned me up against a corner for a minute. And she dragged her knitting chair away from the fire. And pulled the dining table and her little bench closer to it. She tipped me off the wall back onto her, and supported me to the bench.

And I laid my head down on that table and

gave up in a pile. I had tried enough, and gotten myself into a situation good enough, that I could survive even if I gave up. Good job.

I think she dripped hot tea on the back of my neck!

"Don't sleep yet, dear. You can sleep soon, but you're still too cold to fall asleep yet. It's not safe. I don't want a popsicle."

I'm not sure when I noticed, but I know I didn't notice right away, she was speaking English.

So I picked my head off her table and she kept me up with talking. "Where are you from?" and "Where are you headed?" and "How did you come to this?" It was good enough conversation for the time being and her house smelled REALLY GOOD! I don't know what it was, but man, it smelled delicious. I realized she was working in the kitchen or something, probably making me some food to keep me alive. I hoped it was that stuff that smelled really good. She must be some kind of great old-world back-woods cook. She finally brought me something. It was poor, but really nice. It was just flour dumplings in some kind of bone broth. She probably didn't have meat often and had to get by on such things. But it was delicious. But it wasn't what I had smelled. She gave me a bit of country beer. I was never a beer drinker, but I gulped at it like a hungry child gulps their chocolate milk. And I felt halfway to a man again. I still hadn't gotten that treat I smelled when I finally figured out what it was. Gingerbread. The whole, entire house smelled of gingerbread. I craved it badly despite being full enough for my condition. I was still a little delirious, but I wasn't rude enough to ask her for her gingerbread. I just waited a while, answered her questions, and tried to show gratitude, until she sent me to bed.

She sent me to her only bed. It was a one-room cabin, did I mention? It only had privacy in the sense that some corners were out of view of other corners. I didn't know what she was going to do about bed situations. Join me? Put herself out by sleeping on the floor? I didn't care. I was too half-dead to be bashful about sleeping with an old lady or be chivalrous about her sleeping less comfortably than me.

I fell asleep feeling both very warm and awkward... and dreaming deeply—of gingerbread.

Finally I was eating my gingerbread men in their gingerbread house. The house was very wholesome and balanced in taste. Wholesome as in it felt complete, it had all the breadiness you need, the right fluff, but the right chew as well, not wholesome like it's so good for you that you can hardly get it down your gullet. But the gingerbread men were such a different gingerbread. They were far sweeter. Not candy sweet, but definitely in the cookie realm, not the bread realm. They would have been a pinch too sweet if it weren't for the heavy spicing. It was a good heavy. It made them exciting, almost shocking to eat. Somewhere in the dream with no clear transition, the way dreams do, the gingerbread men were alive and did not want to be eaten anymore. But I was eating them anyway because they were delicious! They tried to escape or fought back, but really it was pointless. Little clumsy legs and fingerless arms don't run and climb very well, and they broke in my hands like nommable little nothings.

I was just conscious enough to notice a

change in my dream, but not in-control enough to stop it and turn it. I could sit as a passenger and watch my sweet dream go the other way.

Now I was a gingerbread man and I was a nommable nothing. It didn't seem so cool anymore. I knew I had to escape the giants at the table. If I fought I would be crumbled like super fresh cookies. If I tried to escape, I would have to do so with clumsy little legs and fingerless arms. I could try little sprints and hiding here and there. But while I could hide from eyes, I smelled so wonderful, there couldn't be any lasting hiding place for me.

I was making my go at it anyway when I wasn't a gingerbread man anymore. I was scurrying and hiding the same way. But I was a me. And I was with friends, and family. And the thing trying to eat us was a giant first, then finally, a great Norwegian troll. And some of us were getting caught. My brother got snatched and eaten by the troll. Not my au pair brother, my true brother from back home in America. I never liked my real brother anyway, but it was terrible to see any person being eaten, and he was... my brother.

Delirious. Trauma.

Plus the stench was insane. Troll stench is cornerstone of the legends, but I wasn't prepared for it. It scrambled your brain with an inescapable vertigo. And the effect on your nose, ugh! While it didn't cause a literal burning, you would fantasize about burning the insides of your nose because the tormentful pain of the hot scorching would be less than the mind-rattling assault on your sense of smell. You had to wonder if it was toxic to inhale.

Suddenly I remembered my au pair brother. He was hiding among us somewhere. We were all scattered willy-nilly around a bunch of rough stone pillars (something like the ancient monoliths and taula stuck in the ground by trolls). I owed my au pair brother a debt to rescue him. I had to get him out even if it meant sacrificing myself. I should try to get as many others out as possible too. My girlfriend. My mom. The rest of my Norwegian family and some friends from other countries too, one girl from Menorca.

I finally stopped thinking about who there was to rescue. I couldn't rescue anyway, I could facilitate escape, if it was possible. I took a shot at distraction. I jumped out of my hide and said, "Here, here! Me, me!" It worked, the drooling ogre turned toward me long enough that some others got farther away during the distraction. And some of them picked up on my idea. When I had to hide, another person jumped out and did the same nonsense. And trolls are stupid, so it forgot the last person it was chasing and went to the other. And in this way we were getting farther away and harder to catch. The only problem is that some people weren't getting their timing right, or some panicked and hid badly. And they were getting caught. And the troll would grab one and toss them in a sack he was dragging. He would capture another and throw them bone-breakingly into an old giant birdcage alongside other skeletons. And some he caught and popped straight into his mouth, so there was no telling what he was going to do. And when he noshed someone straight away he really liked to masticate down on the bones good. If you hate the sound of teeth grinding, you must never hear the sound of a troll chewing through human bones. Shudders started going through us and we nearly all lost our timing and composure as "Grrrreeeet, grrrreeet, grrreeet." And if you can get your mind past that sound your mind just runs straight into the smashing offense of his smell. You want to stab your own ears and stick Bunsen burners in your nostrils while you puke your guts out, all over your worthless shoes that can't run you away from this mind-grinder. And when you fight through the sensory storm for anger and pride and sheer will to survive, to get to have one clear thought in your gray mush that used to be a brain, you just come to the realization that half of your friends and family have already been captured or "Gr-rrreeeeet, grrrreeeeet, grrreeeet" by Mr. Troll. And your anger and pride and will-to-survive all give way to despair. This is where I was in my dream. Thinking how if I got away I would still have to come back because I think that quiet guy tossed in the cage was my au pair brother. And I was fed up with this hell challenge and decided I had better wake up to end my dream. And the little tiny, conscious bit of my sleeping brain wrestled with that mad, addictive id bit

that has to keep watching the horrible movie...
and I finally came a little awake.

The fire was still burning in the cabin. I was
surprised that it wasn't out yet. I kept my eyes
closed, but I could still tell the room was lit.
I didn't want to open my eyes. I was still exhausted and I wanted to fall back asleep again
as soon as possible, except that I didn't want
to fall back into that dream. I didn't want the
old woman to see me open my eyes and try to
talk to me. I wasn't ready for that. And I didn't
want to see her in bed with me. I really wasn't
ready for that. So I just kept my eyes closed,
pretended to be comfortable, tried to be comfortable, as I tried to mentally sweep my brain
pan clean of all the nasty filth so I could dream
something nice, like just regular inanimate gingerbread. It still smelled good in the house.

It wasn't working. Every time I tried to fall
back into sleep mode, there was still a little of
troll horror left over. Plus I thought I heard low
talking. Who could this old hag (she was really
quite sweet in my mind still at that time, I'm
blending my current memory with the "then"),
who could this old woman be talking to? Now

I had to see. So I warmed up my eyelids. It's an art and can't be done recklessly. You want to naturally get aimed, hopefully without moving, or move very naturally if you have to, and creepy-crawl peep the eyelids open, just so that you can kind of see through your eyelashes, but no one can see your eyes showing through. Y'know, fake sleeping, like you did when you were a kid. So help me god, that creepers-crone was sitting across the dining table, leaning close to keep her voice low, talking to a six-and-a-half-foot dark figure, like a... she quietly got up, came over as if to tuck me in and I didn't wake up again that night. But as my eyes dropped heavily closed, I thought I heard that wolf say, "Hello again, friend... and goodnight."

When I did wake up I wasn't in a bed. I was on a pile of hay. In a large cage, that did not seem to be in the cabin the night before. And she was cooking.

She fed me well. Sweet things, like gingerbread and candy and a variety of hot chocolates. Savory things like dumpling soups and vegetable pies, but nothing with meat. Clearly I was the meat. For all I knew the soups were flavored with the bones of the last fool who got lost here. Or the bones of all those missing children, dogs, and goats. I didn't want to eat, not just because I might be a cannibal by doing so, but I knew she was fattening me up. I knew she would share me with that cursed, two-faced wolf. The food was delicious, smelled sinfully good, but I meant to say "no." I meant to kick it in her face and starve to death. It would be a hard way to go, to starve to death with food right before me, but it would be worth it to not reward this evil female and her pet friend. Anything to fight for right. But it didn't matter what I decided while I brooded sourly in my little cage, when the food was served there wasn't even a battle of will, I was nothing but an appetite, just a stomach with hands for throwing it in, and a mouth to be the gateway. Every inch of me was made to eat. It's like the smell smelled good to my soul, and I hungered from the depths of my toes. I needed her food and would not be without it if it burned in my belly like orange coals. However I might set my mind in one hour, she had my will in a minute and could force me to beg for it she chose to. No.

She knew she didn't need to play games. And tormenting my soul wouldn't fatten me faster. In fact the stress would probably be bad for me, make me tough, or hurt my appetite. So instead of taunting my helpless will, she cooed like a dove and told me sweet things. She was a sweet, nurturing, evil, old b****.

I could see my belly swelling easily. I looked on nervously every day fearing that my wrists were getting thicker and my fingers were getting chubbier. I started to prepare.

If you don't know what I started to prepare, then you haven't read your way through faery tales like I have. But that's alright. I read them. And I knew what to do. Maybe.

When someone gets caught and fattened in a faery tale, witches ask for a finger to do a pinch test, see if the person is getting chubby. And the witches are all nearly blind so the people, usually kids, stick out objects instead of fingers. And this works. It delays the butchering of the hero who uses this extra time... for nothing actually. The hero always escapes in a way that has nothing to do with the extra time.

But you sit in a cage with an old lady who's

going to butcher you and see if you think any more clearly. Oh, and remember that there's always chunks of bone in your soup that definitely aren't chicken.

I know it's too much like a story. I knew it was too much like a story. But I was so used to delirium by then. I had stopped trying to wake up in my au pair house. I'd even given up on waking up to my last breaths in the frozen forest. It just made me feel the least delirious to live out the story.

I found an old nail in my cage. And when that bag of bones came and asked me to stick out my finger, it confirmed all my predictions. I stuck out the nail instead. She pinched it and she was furious and she screamed, "You're still as hard as nails! A youngster I suppose. A young appetite is hard to fatten. Well, I didn't want to wait, but you'll taste better in the end anyway. *More food!*" She particularly screeched when she said "more food." Shivers ran down my spine as I knew the effect of her food and that I wouldn't be able to will myself not to eat it. I felt so owned and helpless, even more so than being in a cage, when she shrieked "more food."

If I wanted to kick the food away when I was on normal rations, I wanted to shove it straight down her own throat when she upped them; how dare she treat me like this? But I felt the same way whenever she brought me my food. I might have missed having a will of my own if I were capable of any other thought than getting those piles of grub in me as quickly as possible, only making sure that it coated my tongue as I scarfed it down with reckless speed.

After a few days... I don't know how many because I didn't count like a smart prisoner might have... she made me stick out my finger again. As decreed by some bizarre author of fate, there was only that one nail in the cage and it was lost now. So the next thing I held out was a bit of old twig. She screeched in a way that would make a banshee blanch, "Aiieeee! You're still as tough as wood! More food, you little beast, more food for you, to be more food for meeee!" My stomach turned six and a half somersaults.

I tried to look for the spell she put on the

food so I could interrupt it. But I saw nothing. I thought of trying to pollute the food with some dirt. Nothing mattered. When the food came I had all total of one thought, to devour that food with the frenzied attention it deserved from a bear out of hibernation. Nor could the frenzy be stopped until my sides were splitting with fullness. And I could do nothing to disgorge myself. I always thought I might gag myself and throw it up, but once fed I could only languor and nap and think a few idly bitter thoughts about what I would do when I came out of my food coma.

My strategy was worrying me. In the old stories the nails and twigs for a finger trick were just to buy time. But I didn't know what I was buying time toward. I had one test left and it didn't matter. The last test is always a bit of candle end. And even though it's not my own chubby finger, the villain is finally satisfied and decides that a candle end represents a good-enough-to-eat boy. I didn't know how long I spent in this (imaginary?) cabin in the woods with only an empty house to be missing from and no one to be calling for me. I was getting to be more sure that I wouldn't survive and I started to feel again like I didn't want to survive. If I broke out of this cage, and this house, I could only trudge back for miles to a home where nothing waited for me, nothing but guilt for not being humble with my girlfriend, not being able to protect my brother, and not being a generally worthwhile human being.

I quasi-woke, crumpled badly in the cage. The heavy stodgings gave me terrible fits of drowsiness. Coupled with a complete hopelessness for my life, it made me pass out in my cage in the most distorted ways. I had sort of fall-stuffed my shoulders into the corner of the cage and the floor, and got a terrible kink in my neck. I woke to the smell of hot, heavy, badly seasoned air, not fragrant like the normal cooking. It was the Big Bad Wolf. He was crouching down by the cage and the "seasoning" I got on that damp warm draft was his doggy-breath. I carefully wriggled myself out of the corner so as not to break my neck in the process. And when I situated out, I wondered if breaking my neck wouldn't have been a better idea. But now the witch was coming up, adjusting her skirts and nudging Big Bad out of the way. She demanded my finger.

I thought of giving her THE finger, but she was blind and the wolf would've only laughed at me more and that made me mad to think about. I fidgeted for a few seconds. I had formed my plan to stick out the candle end like I was supposed to. But in faery tales there's not another witness in the room. And the candle end never works anyway. So now I had a dilemma of whether to stick out the candle or my real finger when the old idea of trying to deal with reality or illusion broke in. What if there is no witch? What if there is no wolf? I've been really sick lately... mentally, of course. But my stomach was so full. Your eyes and your belly can't hallucinate different things at the same time, can they? I realized I was taking a long time to respond to her. She started screaming at me. I thrust my hand in my pocket and put out the candle bit and didn't look at the wolf.

She, who smelled of urine and bed-ridden even while her house still smelled like gingerbread, she pinched her fingers into the wax.

"He feels funny," she hiss-whined in that voice I had come to hate like pine needles being jammed into my eardrums.

"Oh nonsense, he'll be delicious, like everything you cook."

I looked at the wolf and he was laughing, with a dog-pant type of laugh. He had seen me stick out the candle and he thought it was funny. I never wanted a shotgun and a wood axe so bad... and also to be on the other side of that cage grate. The wolf said he was going out to invite the others then.

The idea of being eaten by a party made me feel weaker than ever. I could feel my flesh weaken with each bite I saw them taking of me.

The hag pulled out the biggest butcher knife I have ever seen, a blade maybe a foot long and four inches broad at the base. I hoped to see her withered old arm tremble with its weight, but she lifted and carried it fine. She started to whet the blade. This was my chance.

"That's not the right way to sharpen a blade. That will never cut," I lied. I knew nothing about sharpening a blade right, but one of the old Norwegian faery tales used this trick. The fool hands the victim the knife to sharpen. The victim sharpens it and slays his captor. I stared at her for her response. I fantasized about taking the knife and cutting off her entire head.

She smiled, "No, I'll do all the work, you just stay tender, sweetheart."

The doting way she said "sweetheart" sank into my bone marrow. I could feel it curdling around in there. The natural affection she said it with made it sound like she could do this with her own grandchildren. Maybe she already had. She hummed away, passing the knife over the whetstone, maybe remembering the old days when she dismembered her own family with it.

She came to open the cage. I started to wonder what I could do. I dug around in my mind, trying to find a memory of a weapon. I tried to use mental projection to search my cage; I desperately needed a tool, but couldn't let her see me preparing to fight. I stared at the ground to look at her. Maybe if she held the knife wrong I could rush her and get around it, disarm her, throw her to the ground and... aaaaaaggggh! It was all no use. Trying to run around a giant knife like that could leave me dead in one wrong step. If only I had a twig and a nail to throw into her eyes. I was furious with desperation. Why had I followed the faery tales?

I decided to play it easy. I tried to play it easy. Maybe something would present itself if I were patient and wary. Maybe some good ol' Hollywood-style trick would save me. But for now, all I could do was to crawl to her command with no confidence. Like a tiny kitten, too little to know what's happening when it gets picked up and too awkward and helpless to avoid it anyway, I went with her. I laid my head on her lap, that kind old stinking murderer's lap. She put that ponderous knife blade against my neck. She wouldn't do it here on her lap, would she? Get my blood all over her skirts? Don't they save the blood to make sausages and puddings in places like this? Don't splatter me here! I gulped, but gulping my neck pushed against the tight-held blade more. And I didn't want my neck to press against the blade more. But now I was infatuated with gulping. I felt the overwhelming need to swallow again and again.

Swallow that lump down my throat before she cuts the lump out.

"Be calm, my darling..."

... she said, in the same way she said it to her tiny little grandchildren some years ago as she became totally corrupt, obsessed with the blood of people, who were all baited with cursed sweet gingerbread.

She worked the knife on my neck just a tiny bit. Something between trying to shave me and trying to cut my skin, just the first few layers. I think she did. I think she got just barely past the first layer, and that I was bleeding, on the knife, and on myself, but not yet on her. No drops, just a smear of blood, starting to gather up enough to run. My own blood, to be had by some cannibal witch and the wolf from story-time hell. And their friends.

Then she blew lightly, straight down on my ear. It didn't smell like doggy breath atleast. It didn't smell like anything. But it made feel the weight of my last feeding again... and... stuffed... and... ... groggy... I... ... faded...

From consciousness.

I woke up in the hospital, with an IV, and alot of other stuff, for frost trauma.

This transition was never resolved for me so I cannot resolve it for you. Here is all I have:

Runa reported me missing. (That's its own mystery right there.) They looked for me where so many had gone missing. They did find not my blood splatter by the bridge, but a dog sniffed me out farther up, in a "snow cave" in the ravine. I didn't have the survival skill of making a snow cave. I think I fell in a snow drift and got lucky.

I don't know how I got there, though.

The police told me I went out and got lost in the woods. They told me I have amnesia. They told me the whole police report and left me nothing to fill in. I tried asking about a house in the woods. They said there is no house and no one lives in the woods. And they didn't ask me for any more information. Police in every country can be so stupid.

The police not asking anything made it easy to put off my dual-reality. I didn't worry about the Big Bad Wolf, or sensory deprivation. Hey, I got lost in the woods, but I was safe now.

What is there to figure out? No need to figure out how long I was really gone for. No sense in checking my weight; nobody knew what weight I was when I left so how could we know if I'd been fattened. Anyway, I was due back for work. My au pair family was back home. And I could take all the time I wanted to find a therapist and tell her my dreams of faery tale witches cutting my head off.

I got out of the hospital. Fresh air. Cold? Sure. Stinging? Yes, but fresh, fresh air. Even home seemed kind of pretty. Maybe I'll be alright.

Then Runa did something terrible. Something clever... and caring... and cruel. She came over to visit.

She called it catching up. She didn't even ask if I was ok, just acted like, of course I was ok. But she stayed there. She stuck on the couch, like improperly socialized glue. Long after things got boring, awkwardly boring, with prolonged periods of silence. But even though she was acting like an oblivious geek, she sensed every time I was about to say, "I'll let you go, then,' and she put in some pointless bit of conversation to string things on a little more. It was like being kidnapped in my own apartment.

But that's the deadly brilliance of what she did. She didn't tell me anything I wasn't ready to hear. And she didn't ask me about anything that I wasn't ready to talk about. She interrupted my hints to leave, ignored my hints to leave. She lingered with dogged persistence, until... the ice broke.

I don't know just what sentence started it. I don't remember what topic bridged that inconceivably gargantuan gap. But somehow the truth came out. Somehow I had the biggest, longest, deepest conversation I ever had about how I feel, and what I believe, and just how crazy I could be inside. If people only knew.

But now she knew.

And the dirty thing is she believed. She believed 100% that I was held prisoner by an unknown witch in the woods. She DIDN'T believe in the Big Bad Wolf and SHE actually had to apologize to ME, for laughing at me.

But I didn't want her to believe me. I wanted to rub my eyes out of this midwinter night's dream. And besides, if it were real, I should be able to remember how I got away. Being found buried in the snow only makes sense if I just got lost and disoriented the normal ol' scientific way. But that stubborn (bit of a witch herself) Runa, insisted on believing me. And what's worse is she made me believe in that man-eating troll at the bridge.

She said it's only real when you believe in it. ~Then why make me believe in it!?~

"Because I can't not believe in it. And I need someone to be with me. I need someone to fight it together. I need to not be alone."

That last line rang in my ears like the heavy, cathedral church bells. When you look at it that way, I left her alone before she ever left me alone.

It's funny, the thing that I disrespected about Runa the most is what made me... don't make me say the "L" word here, but you get the picture. I didn't like that she believed in everything; I thought it was the biggest flaw in her personality. Even when she was believing me! ... I didn't want her to believe me; I wanted her to be coldly skeptical, tell me it was all in my head and the best thing was therapy or some drug treatment to get it out of my head. (I don't like taking drugs; I would refuse to take psychiatric ones. It's just what I wanted to be told.) But it bonded me to her. And that bond was... "L" word stuff. That pretty target of infatuation became the person I wanted to be with for the rest of my life. This was the flaw that made her perfect.

But it also meant that moving forward wasn't going to have psych-therapy. Not yet. I kept thinking I'd get therapy soon. Even if I was falling in "L" with my kooky girlfriend, she was still crazy and I couldn't let her take me mentally down with her. Anyway, for just now I decided to go along and... fight the troll, or fight to get rid of the troll or something bananas in that vein.

It didn't help at all that Runa, whose idea it was to confront this problem, wouldn't go anywhere near the troll at all. I started to feel like she was tackling the problem by making me solve it. It didn't make me mad exactly, but you know, that lack-of-respect issue I had with her...

I declared that I was going to get a group of police to go to the area with me and search the area for a missing object from when I got lost. But really... *wink wink* ... I would be tricking them into hunting for the troll.

"That won't work at all," Runa told me, "but you do that. It's important for you to try your own ideas in the solution. It will get you closer."

I felt so condescended. "L" feelings don't make everything happy, kids.

But she had given me permission for my "useless" idea so I decided to take my shot and maybe prove her *wrong*.

I was trying to think of what to lie to the police about that I was missing. Maybe I could say I lost my camera and that it might have useful records for evidence. I spent no less than ten minutes practicing this scenario in my head before I realized... I was missing my phone. I lost it. While I was lost. I forgot because when I woke up in the cage without my phone, I decided that the witch and the wolf stole it.

See? Now that I was back in the real world, I had this kind of "optional" perception of reality. I felt like I could choose whether I was in the house in the woods, or not, like a Schrödinger's cat. Does this make sense to you? Real reality was so weird (gyah, this is so hard to explain): ok it's like dreaming a realistic dream and then waking up and trying to finish what you were doing in the dream, but you can't because realistic dream wasn't reality. But it's also like being partly awake while you dream and you can control the dream some. But it's also like not being sober in reality when things are going wrong. All of these mind states at the same time! Anyway, my phone was truly gone and because of my particular brain damage, that fact was a complete surprise to me. Did I mention delirium?

I wondered to myself if the missing phone was proof that I really got kidnapped. But it's not, is it? When you're found unconscious in the snow, anything could have happened to your phone. I thought of arguing about it to Runa, but she already believed everything I said no matter what. Damn pretty little nut job. *sigh* She was even trying to believe the Big Bad Wolf part. What do you do with somebody this unhinged? "L" word!

I went to the police station, told them that I was missing my phone, and that they should send a patrol of officers with me to hunt for it since it could have valuable evidence. Keep in mind that these people were not Runa. They would not believe I was kidnapped and weren't terribly worried about the evidence of me getting lost in the snow. Fortunately they kind of wanted that record in case there was something to learn from it to prevent further such "accidents." ... They sent one officer with me.

Two guys and one 9mm pistol against a troll. What could go wrong?

There's a strange camaraderie in doing something pathetically hopeless with another person. Two guys. Searching the woods. For a cell phone. He came with a small handheld metal detector. And I came with ulterior motives, psychosis residue, and still no sensibility for the great outdoors. Atleast he didn't know all this about me. All he knew is that my Norwegian was pretty sh**. (How old are my readers?) Anyway, my Norwegian was better by now, but pretty low. But you know what? He felt stupid being given the assignment. I felt stupid dragging him on it. It made us laugh together. A tiny little brotherhood of putzes.

I started to feel extremely guilty that I was trying to set him up to fight a troll with a pea shooter.

It doesn't matter because we didn't have to kill the troll, we just needed to discover it. That pistol could just discourage the troll enough that we could escape and call for backup. I'm not sure what the "heavy" armed response is for a small Norwegian mountain town, probably a lot less than the infamously militarized American police forces. But a few shotguns and hunting rifles can bring down a bridge troll, probably, right?

You can bet I was checking my escape route all the time. This time I was running away toward home, NOT the middle of the g**d*** woods for round two with the family-eating psycho granny.

But it really doesn't matter because that fear was probably all just nonsense. This was just the first step in me finding a therapist. The cop and I will find nothing. I'll tell Runa she's wrong and a little crazy. She'll be mad, oh of course. But maybe if I tell her with a great back-rub and hot chocolate and I'm super support-ive, she won't dump me again. And we'll live happily ever after. Mmm, faery tale ending, so to speak.

At some point in this fiasco, Haugen (the cop) and I had to do some kind of searching. I had to pretend I really wanted to find my phone. (You're probably assuming that of course I really wanted to find my phone, but no. I can hardly explain, but normal social in-terests and adulting responsibilities just had no weight on my mind after a couple weeks of delirium. Did I mention the delirium?) And Haugen had to pretend that there was hope for finding a cell phone in the snow with a metal detector that was not meant for finding cell phones buried in snow; it was really like one of those security wands.

Haugen sure was giving it to me. Not mean like; he was the friendliest cop I ever met in my life. Just non-stop teasing about my pathetic Norwegian, worse memory, and worst sense of direction.

Oh, I forgot to mention that the bridge was

there. Rebuilt. City must have redone it while I was "out" I guess. Kind of. It's hard to tell things in a story like this. I'll explain in a bit.

I was having a blast with Haugen, teasing him back. But after too much of this, I started to get annoyed. I was probably hangry. I hadn't eaten right for going on an all-day ordeal. After waiting around at the police station for a meeting, and waiting for them to get an officer briefed and ready, and meandering in the woods, I was overdue for lunch. I noticed I was off when I started cussing at Haugen in my head for not using that "metal detector" seriously.

Then I remembered that I didn't care about finding my phone. I was just looking for a goddamn troll. It was a need, my only need, or the core of all my needs atleast. I had to find out if I needed to learn how to fight supernatural monsters or spend thousands of dollars on therapy. Is that beautiful girl I was falling in love with some brilliant and misunderstood creature, inspired by the most subtle forces in the universe... or in denial about her own needs for therapy? The only use for a phone would've been that if there was a battle between Haugen and a Norwegian bridge troll, it'd be great to get that clip and post it online. But I wasn't thinking any such things at the time. I was thinking bitter, petty thoughts about that loser cop Haugen.

A darker thought occurred to me. What if my irritability wasn't hunger? It was anxiety? My ulterior motives were eating through my armor of humor and biting me in the back. I was afraid of what I was doing and I couldn't admit it to myself; I was too defensive, being so busy hiding it from Haugen. I'm not playing with his life, am I? This is all out of my control. Isn't it?

Acid flared in my stomach. My anger and exasperation raged more, but I turned the anger back on myself, where it belonged. Cowardice has made every part of this harder. I was trying to trick Haugen into fighting my battle for me. If I wanted to resolve this I would have to be brave and go to that bridge myself. Either that or go home, stick my head under a pillow and avoid everything forever. Probably give up on Runa. Maybe give up on Norway.

I wasn't ready for that much quitting. I

stopped trying to manipulate Haugen to cross the bridge. I went to the bridge myself.

My vision flickered so bad I thought I was having a seizure. The bridge would flicker to its old ruins. Then back again. A trail from something gigantic would flicker in the snow. Then disappear. Haugen seemed far, far away. I started to see things like a dragonfly does. All these tiny pictures came in and made a mosaic. But they didn't align. Half of my thousand eyes saw the bridge rebuilt there. Many eyes saw it missing and in ruins. Some of my eyes saw pieces of the wolf's fur, the witch's dress, people scattering from the troll in the dream. I looked for one basic reality. I stared at the snow. All my eyes filled with white. Nobody questioned that the snow was really there. Pure, simple. My head rolled back on my neck. Sounds were flickering too. The snoring. Flicker out. The wolf and the witch whispering. Flicker on. Runa. Aksel. Poor, poor Aksel. His voice before. His voice before he stood... no waited, *fetal*. Balled up right where I'm standing. I slid my foot on the tough snow. Toward the bridge. I was getting tense, I felt swollen with blood pressure. I wanted a confrontation. My troll, or my hallucinations are going to have a very big fight. And whichever it is, Haugen is about to get the show of his life because I am flipping out.

I wanted to run over the bridge, but I had to go slow in case it wasn't there. Flicker in. Flicker out. I stuck my hand in the snow covering the railing. I needed all my balance. I had to get to the edge of one reality and stick my foot out over the other reality and see if it was there.

Leaning away from my own feet. Ignoring whatever Haugen was shouting at me. This is how I approached the critical point of the bridge.

Finally, breathing like I finished a 6-mile run, I got to the old edge. Ruins and new bridge kept flickering on and off. And still images of the gingerbread cabin, and that dream, the smell. Ogh! The smell of the troll! It was in my nose now. I wanted to cry and sneeze to flush that smell out. I pushed my foot past the edge. But it wasn't enough pressure to be sure. I hit my foot up and down, up and down on the new rebuilt bridge.

It was there! My foot kept hitting! It made crunchy thumps as it landed on gritty snow over solid bridge. I committed my weight to the step. I wasn't falling. None of my realities were falling. I was safe, and halfway sane, when the shout arose from underneath; it was like standing in a belfry when the bell is rung. In archaic sounding, but perfectly understandable Norwegian, I heard, "Pay the toll!"

With one hand and two steps the bridge troll came from under the bridge and straddled the mid-level of the large ravine while leaning to the bridge.

He only had two noses. Each one was longer than the rest of his head. But not so big as to hide his tiny green-gray eyes. He was bald with a gray remainder of hair, much older than the troll dolls I saw in the tourist shops. He had warts all over, bigger than my own head. He was bluish as from the cold, but the rest of his tint made it seem jaundiced too. His teeth were a rotting mess of orange and green and empty pits. That's probably where the smell came from.

I felt a poop coming out of my bottom and I

was sure to lose control of it soon. I ran to cross the bridge.

Now something very peculiar happened. He dropped his hand to block off the way and then swept it in to catch me. I think he started the movement before I started running. Now everything happened so fast I really can't tell, but I think my muddled reality messed with me. I think part of me saw the hand coming at me as just a hallucination. I was just trying my hardest to run my fastest and will my way past the hallucination. And the troll probably didn't expect anyone to run to his hand so his catch timing was delayed. I sprinted and jumped like I was clearing a gap. He slapped forward and clasped to catch me. But I bounced off of his palm before his fingers closed and got bounced away like a ball that a little kid doesn't know how to catch. Except I got bounced hard and I'm not rubber. It felt like every organ in me smashed against every bone inside of me. I landed in a stunned and useless heap.

If you've never been hurt badly (I mean in the vitals: the guts, the spine, the head (broken limbs is a different experience)), the first thing you think to yourself is that it's just pain. It's just pain and all you need to do is shake off the pain, get up, and do what needs doing. But when you make that first move to stand up, in defiance of the meaningless pain, your body tells you something else: that your back won't hold you, your head won't steer the ship, or your chest won't even give you air to breathe. And you collapse, kind of desperately, careful not to move anymore and trigger more pain and damage. You feel almost apologetic to your own body. "I'm sorry I didn't respect you. I'm sorry I didn't understand your pain." But the pain isn't what's really important. What's important is that the fear of the pain told you to give up. It told you everything is finished, there's nothing you can do. I only felt this way once before. Then my life wasn't in danger; I was just going to lose at sports. This time a troll, so strong that he could knock me 20 feet on accident, was coming to likely finish me off. I was trying to get comfortable with death. I was there, in a deformed version of the fetal position, my face cut on some scratchy snow, bleeding a little streamlet. That streamlet burned the only part of my face that felt anything. The rest was numb. I took tiny, tiny breaths that still nearly bust my ribs and back with the pressure. The troll could eat me how he liked. I had nothing left to fight with and I just needed the inevitable pain to stop.

The troll shouted as he stomped out of the ravine to my flesh heap. This time I couldn't understand most of it, only, "No, no, NO! Blah blah blah, money, blah blah."

My left arm could move. Some section of my brain, that wasn't distorted with concussion and pain, remembered what money was. Without me really making any decision, my left arm started moving around, almost on its own, like a severed tentacle. It wriggled around my body. Nothing else on me could move. It dug into my money pocket. And got a grip on my money just as...

The troll picked me up by an ankle. He was crushing my ankle, but it really didn't matter at this point. I swung upside down past his face. My barely working head was flooding blood. My left hand flung money at his face. He didn't even blink at it. His eyes didn't even track the movement as the money fell. And I could swear one of the coins bounced off a nose and into his eye. This crooked, corrupt, evil stinking troll was going to ignore the fare just so he could eat me!

I foresaw him swinging me and finishing me off on one of his rocks. I would be the next splatter. Just another one. But all of the rocks were covered by snow. Maybe he would use one of the trees.

Suddenly I started to fight like everything on me worked because in one more second the pain could be all gone. I kicked and screamed. I punched the air. I hollered for Haugen to, "Shoot him! Shoot him! What are you waiting for?!"

The tree idea must have been the right one. I saw the troll look square at a tree and then straight at me. He brought his arm back hard for the swing. Too hard. He must've thought he had a better grip on me because as he whipped back I came rip slipping out of his fingers, sailing through the air again to crash into a hardened bank of snow. I got up and tried to run. I couldn't run, but I hobbled like a demon. That is until Haugen grabbed me and started dragging me like I was a sled. I howled for him to drag faster, in a frantic panic about the huge troll chasing us down.

* * *

Haugen reported nothing about a troll. I tried to catch him confidentially. To see if he was covering the real story because people would think we were crazy, (but really he could join our inner circle with Runa and I and become one of the troll hunters). No. Nothing of the sort.

Officer Haugen reported that I started acting funny when I got to the place of the missing bodies. He said that I walked erratically, shouted bizarrely and jumped back off the bridge. His report is that I then climbed a tree and threw myself out of that. I tried running away though clearly injured. He tackled me and dragged me toward safety until I had calmed down and he was too exhausted to continue. When I said, "Shoot it, shoot it!" he thought I was talking about a black bear that was moving in a bush nearby.

"What about the distances. How did I jump

20 feet the first time, and more than 40 the second?!"

"Well, they were quite good jumps, but I don't think they were that big."

"What about these injuries?" My right arm was broken in several places. My ankle wasn't broken, but was remarkably bruised. I had a concussion, possibly multiple. And maybe worst of all, my organs looked like I had been in a high-speed car collision.

"Well, yes! You were throwing yourself against boulders hidden in the snow, you maniac. You're lucky; you know in Norway, they say that some of the old boulders are really trolls and they'll eat you if you're not careful."

They (hospital, police, host family) told me it's ok. They told me maybe I feel guilt and trauma about what happened to Aksel. They told me they made an appointment for me with a therapist so that I wouldn't try to hurt myself anymore.

Well, I was right about my troll hunt being the first step to therapy.

I told Runa about that lying bastard, Haugen. Runa said he wasn't lying. She said that he's just like me. What!?! I said that I never lied about what I saw or didn't see. Runa said that when your brain can't accept something, it turns it into the nearest thing it can accept. Haugen's brain actually saw me jumping much smaller distances and all on my own. His brain changed all the visual information into something it could understand. It's called Gestalt psychology.

If I get one more hole in my sense of reality, I don't think I'll survive. I imagine my brain having bruises and bleeding like my organs. ... ...

Nobody who has the right to shoot guns believes in the troll. Most of the people who believe in the troll are children and a few unarmed weirdos. To fight the troll we need more belief. How do we make belief?

Strength in numbers. Groupthink.

I had a plan. The same bigger plan. More police. More believers. More risk. More results.

I hope.

As I lay in the hospital healing my fragmented innards, with Runa holding my hand and pretending I don't smell like hospital bed (I remembered the witch smell), I told her my new plan.

Let's make a big, city event to get everyone to the bridge. We need the city to reclaim it. Have a ground-breaking ceremony to rebuild the bridge, new police patrols. It should be easy because this missing children thing became a national issue. It changed the way people were parenting. It bent the culture. EVERYONE needed this problem solved. Not just Runa and I.

Of course the mayor and dignitaries would be up front. The police in large force, both for civil image, and also as a symbol of reclaiming this place from the cults or psychos who were allegedly terrorizing the community. Then, also as a symbol of our new made safety, a local preschool class. These would be our believers. Plus some local religious types, politically, to counter the bad religious stigma of the cultists, but really because I hoped they would believe more easily than the secular crowd. And to round it all out, several of Runa's acid-tripping druggie friends. We toyed seriously with dosing the cops with LSD to really help them see the troll, but decided that actual hallucinations combined with real make-believe monsters (I don't know how to phrase that, I'm not a writer) might end up with innocent people getting shot. No LSD.

Or course the risk to all of this was the tiny schoolchildren seeing the troll and getting stomped into blood wine by him, while the adults, including the armed ones, all hallucinate Haugen-style that the kids are just playing hide-n-seek or something.

When I said this out loud to Runa, and used the word hallucinate for what Haugen did, it triggered another problem. If the troll was really real. Then his bridge was real. Which means the ruins is a hallucination. What happens when they try to build a bridge where there's an invisible bridge already?

Runa said it's not that one belief is real and the other belief is wrong. (I feel like Schrödinger's cat is clawing around inside my head.) Runa explained what's important is that people who don't believe in the troll can be made to believe for long enough to save everyone who does believe in it.

Somehow the world will work out the ambiguous existence of that bridge later.

And then... Runa got going. While I suffered in the hospital, that girl emailed and flyered and did town hall rants. She rallied people like a political professional. (She's actually the hotel clerk.) She orchestrated every part of that scheme just like we planned it. If someone second guessed the presence of the police, she convinced them; a preschool class, the same thing. In the spring, when the snow was fully melted and the wilderland turning bud-green, ready to be bursting with flowers, the city too was ready to be reborn. And it was all Runa. Even when I got the pieces of my guts together enough that they let me out of the hospital, I wasn't much help.

The day of the event I was sick with anticipatory guilt. I never really got over what I let happen to Aksel. I just don't talk about it all the time. If get a class of adorable preschool children devoured... I have to go die alone in the woods because I can't live with that. I kept making Runa promise me the kids were going to be really, really far back. She promised me that she handled it. But I had to leave her alone. Her nerves were worse than mine. I started to notice a smell. People used to always say that dogs can smell fear. I wonder if people can smell fear if it's strong enough. Maybe if they believe.

The spot for the preschool class was pretty far back. I decided to position myself in front to help them run. Runa couldn't. They agreed to not make her speak in the ceremony, but because of her tremendous activity in the cause they expected her to be central. The preschool class came late. Everyone smiled at the little cuties. I deliberately didn't look at how cute they are. I just stood there like a guardian, a random stranger guardian.

The ceremony started and some kids were whimpering already. The teacher was hushing them. She was used to random crying behavior from kids. She didn't know that they could hear the snoring, or smell that smell.

The big shots cut a ribbon. They went to break ground. The spade hit the dirt.

It was a different experience to see the troll this time. He was far away still. There's an aura, a bubble of violence if you will. If you've ever known an angry person, had someone aggressively contemptuous in your life, then you know exactly what I mean: that particular range where you're inside their hate, the place you most don't want to be. And if you've never had such a person in your life I'm not sure I can explain it to you. But in the simplest terms it includes fear, confusion, and being insecure of your version of reality. A perpetually angry person can feel just as imaginary as the Big Bad Wolf.

The bridge troll roared a roar that shook leaves out of the trees. Now the children were in hysterics. The roar expanded his bubble. No adults heard it, except for Runa and I. None knew why the children were crying.

The kids could see now. The troll was much fatter and older than I had noticed before. I suppose he was maybe hundreds of years old. But I mean he looked like a 60-year-old man. His belly wasn't as big as it could have been, maybe shrunk with winter hibernation. But it still looked great and heavy, like he could eat a whole bear with ease. His arms looked all saggy.

His limbs, while huge in every measurement, still didn't look thick enough for that humpty-dumpty body with that ponderous head (plus the oversized noses). But when he moved, something remarkable happened. The layers of flab disappeared over emerging sinews, like a transformer robot moving outer shells aside and revealing all the gears and hydraulics beneath.

It was so silly, a fat troll having muscles like a comic book drawing, it made me think of stories, and cartoons, and for a second he disappeared. I guess I didn't believe in him for a moment. And I was this close to deciding not to believe in him anymore; let everyone else work it out on their own. I saw the cute little kids crying and bawling. I thought, "Kids imagine things. They need to learn that the monster under the bed isn't real and this is how they learn."

Flicker in. Flicker out.

And I saw him coming out of the ravine...

Flicker out. Flicker in.

Runa was there. I lost my choice to not believe.

It doesn't matter, I'm not the one who needs to believe. It has to be them, normal people. People who haven't gone crazy with sensory deprivation and almost been eaten by a witch and the Big Bad Wolf in their dreams. People who don't rub mystic crystals while they're praying in church. Plain. Responsible. Adults.

And I thought Runa would maybe be doing some kind of hero duty and herding the kids to safety. No. When I saw her, she was just looking at me, waiting for me. To act.

"What about the kiiddds?!" said one of us.

She stared like a deer in headlights.

I yelled to the kids to run, run all the way home. Their teacher gave me the dirtiest look. The children jumped up and started huddling and moving away, but they didn't really run. They needed the teacher's permission. I tried to scare them away myself, but they weren't scared of me. They could see a giant, two-nosed troll climbing out of the ravine. I was nothing.

Runa's druggie hippie friends watched me try to scare the kids. They got all mortified and indignant. A couple of them ran over to stop "the bully." One started yelling at me. The other read more on the kids' faces. She saw that I wasn't the bully. She looked for what was scaring the kids. She really looked. She screamed.

Too slow. The troll was taking his first steps toward people. He ignored all those clueless dignitaries who were closest to him.

One after another, hippies started screaming. But it was taking too long for people to see. He covers a lot of ground in one step and he was just a few steps away.

He picks up the dirtiest looking hippie and stuffs him in a bag on his belt. He kicks one of the clean-looking hippies like a two-year-old kicks a soccer ball. I guess he likes food with an earthy smell?

The religious people were all looking around in confusion and finally one of them saw it. Still the others stared through while that one among them pointed out the danger in desperate, silent terror.

The troll seemed excited about the kids. He went for them.

At last, the school teacher, absorbed something, out of love, out of devotion, out of a teacher's bond with HERS, she could see.

Flicker in.

She let out a scream that vibrates my nerves to this day, "It'ssss aaaa trollllllllll!!!"

My ears split with the piercing wrenching hurt of that scream, but my heart sprang with hope. One officer saw it. He pulled his gun. He shot. I don't know how many of the other officers saw it or just pulled and started shooting the same direction because of copthink, but soon there was a thrilling hope of bullet storm flying at that nasty child-eating, dog-killing beast.

I don't know. I couldn't tell if the bullets bounced off him or passed through like a ghost. But nothing hurt him. Why? He was real enough now. People could see him. Dozens of normal, responsible adults could see him. All that's left is for the troll to die.

Right?

Then the problem got much more severe. His face changed from hungry to furious. His tiny eyes almost disappeared inside his scowl. His bushy nose hair blew out in big angry huffs. His swollen, pock-marked lips sneered over his green and orange teeth. He became the ancient, disgusting legend of manslaughter.

He started for the officers now. They had been too busy shooting to move away. I saw poor Haugen get flung like I had been flung. But Haugen hit a tree and it broke his back. Haugen!

Still, most of the dignitaries were safe in utter bewilderment at what was going on. Still not believing. Too disconnected to feel the common reality. Other innocent people were getting crushed, flung and bit.

Then the troll picked up one of the preschoolers by the head. He obviously meant to eat the kid, but he squeezed the child's head too hard. The head popped and fell out of the troll's grip. The body of the child dropped to the ground with a mangled mush flopping around at the top of the neck.

My soul could have left me and never returned after seeing that...

I took an involuntary moment of silence. I started to lie down to mourn in guilt. The snow was melted, but the ground was icy cold, maybe just cold enough that I could pass away.

But there was so much to do. I'm not a hero, but I couldn't let him get more kids. Kids have to grow up with healthy trauma or something; they can't die.

The troll forgot about the first kid and went after more. Most of them were hiding behind trees atleast. The teacher was trying to help them. I remembered the dream. I tried screaming and waving my arms to attract the troll toward me. It wasn't working. I thought maybe because I was screaming "Aagh!" with an American accent. But then I realized it didn't matter because, duh, people were screaming EVERYWHERE.

I remembered that trolls have a thing about Christians. I thought about yelling, "I´m a Christian!" But that was a total lie. What if the troll could magically sense the truth? Supposedly they smell the blood of Christians. I pointed to the religious group, actually all Christian, just Lutheran and Catholic. I yelled in my best Norwegian, "LOOOK! Christians!!"

The Christians gaped at me in horror, frozen for a few seconds by me selling them out. But I was trying to save the children!

It worked. The troll whipped his head, stared for a second, sniffed the air, and bumble rushed to the Christians. He caught two of the Christians panicking together. He held them between both hands, interlocked his fingers and brought his elbows up to squish and grind with all his might. He pressed them like he was cooking regular kitchen food, not living humans in their last hideous moments. Other Christians sprinted behind trees. One was trying to burrow into old snow. The troll kicked a tree that a priest was hiding behind. He kicked it like he meant to knock the tree over and kill him. The tree held up, but was shaken enough to knock the priest's head and sprawl him unconscious on the ground that instant.

The troll grabbed the choir leader who was trying to burrow. He bit at the old church lady's head. She put her arms out in defense and he only bit into her arms.

One arm came off clean but the other didn't. He worked her around a little and got through the arm, but some of the yarn of her sweater was still holding on. He opened his teeth a little to unpinch the yarn, but the whole forearm came out and dangled by the sweater. The fore-arm and hand slowly sliding out of their portion of the sweater. But before that could happen he bit again and pulled away and broke the sweater yarn this time. Then he started chewing. The air was filled with that "grrreeet, grreeet."

I forgot all about trying to solve any catastrophes as the sound grated through my skin, wormed in my muscle, chewed on my nerves, and scraped my bones. It was exactly like the dream. Human bones being chewed by teeth is the most disgusting sensation in all of reality or make-believe.

The troll spotted another person making a run for it. He threw the rest of the church lady at the runner. (She had stopped screaming and gone into shock by then). The troll missed, but that unnerving missile startled the runner into falling over in the mud. (Melting snow leaves behind alot of mud.) The troll ran and pounced, not like a cat, like a 4-year-old. And he slapped down on both bodies in the mud. The mud might have cushioned them enough to stay alive. But his strength was epic and it most likely just gave them a slow death of being mostly crushed, but not flattened.

But the children were gaining ground. Not much, but it was working. I had sacrificed old religious people for the young. And people were screaming less. He rushed at two slower kids. I tried to distract him, but I screamed too late. He caught one in each hand. He swung them out and back in, banging their poor heads together. Then he gulped one after the other. It looked like he was swallowing pills except he licked his nasty lips after.

I saw the police finally hiding in cover. I yelled at them to shoot and jump back to hiding. I didn't care if they could hurt the troll. I just wanted the behemoth to get distracted from the kids. They didn't want to shoot because their guns weren't working. I was trying to yell at them about the strategy of misdirection, in English since I figured the troll couldn't understand English. I thought I heard one of the officers calling the military when... in one whirlwind zoom blur of motion I was in that sack on the troll's belt. Next to the dirty hippy and some fat cop and maybe someone else. It smelled of urine and feces. I blamed the others, but I couldn't be sure it wasn't my own filth. I heard gunshots, more shrieks, and that horrible grreet grrreeet. Then in the noise and stench and all the body weight smashing me, I passed out.

I woke up in a cage, a bone basket cage. My limbs were twisted into an inhuman position. I slowly unwrought my poor bent joints, nearly paralyzed by pain as I tried. Nothing seemed broken, in my arms and legs anyway, just some ribs. He probably broke my ribs when he picked me up. Or it could have been being squashed with all those other bodies in his heinous people purse. I knew broken ribs from my last encounter. I wouldn't be able to breathe right for days. I tried not to move while I looked around. I surveyed my plight. It was a cave, lit only by one fire. A few carcasses lay scattered without method. I could see the broken remnants of a rusted old iron cage on the ground. I examined the loosely bonded basket of bones holding me. I could get out of it, probably. I just wouldn't get very far, if he were awake. Now if he were asleep... I was in the cage with the dirty hippie and a quietly sobbing nun. The officer must have died from shock or abuse. He was laid out on the ground. The troll didn't seem interested in him.

My mental inventory rattled on in spite of my physical pain, in fact, strategizing seemed to numb the pain. The troll evidently didn't turn to stone in sunlight, unless cloud cover is enough to protect him. He's invulnerable to bullets. Maybe because he doesn't believe in them. Do we need a knight with a lance to impale him, because he can believe in that? But in the stories, knights never kill trolls. Ever. Ever. It's always a trick. Trolls die from tricks. People challenge them sometimes. I don't have any troll tricks. I don't know if this troll will fall for the old story ones. Sometimes a kid squeezes cheese and it freaks out the troll because the kid says the cheese is rocks. OK, so should I challenge a troll to a rock squeezing contest or run away when he sleeps? What if he eats me before he sleeps? I can wait for him to take me out of the cage and then challenge him. If he falls asleep first, I can "run" away. But if I run away, this goes on forever. If I beat him... Why is the one person farthest from troll culture the troll battler? How did this happen? Why not a Norwegian? Why did I have to believe? ... I believed for Love. Stupid Runa. Stupid, pure, beautiful, believe in everything and believe in me too, Runa.

"I challenge you!"

No response. He just kind of twitches an ear at me. I shake the hippie. "Tell him in old-style Norwegian, that I challenge him."

The hippie does. The troll stops fiddling his faddles and looks at us.

The hippie looks inquisitively at me, "Challenge him to what? Chess?"

"A challenge of strength." I'm operating on instinct and auto-pilot here. Right after I answered, the other part of my brain kicked in and said (to itself), "Could I have challenged him to chess? That would be way easier than a challenge of strength. You idiot!"

But the hippie is already translating. And I can tell by his tone that he's giving it some gusto, playing it good. I can kind of understand when the hippie talks because he's probably bad at speaking old-time Norwegian. I can't understand a word when the troll speaks, but his laughter makes it clear enough. A challenge of strength with me must be a joke to him.

But the hippie is running with it, he doesn't consult me, he plays it good, "You've been challenged! You don't accept?"

My internal brain is reassuring myself, "I couldn't play him a board game, he doesn't believe in board games. Atleast he wouldn't believe in any that I know how to play. It doesn't matter that I can't win at strength with him. The whole point is that it's a trick. A more impossible trick is a better trick... "

The troll roars his answer so hard that I reel back in the cage. His eyes fire up like he's about to rip the cage off its rope—(Did I mention we were hanging from the ceiling? A suspended cage.)—and throw it against the wall. I grab at the bones trying to brace myself as the troll stands up. My heart beats so loud I can hear it. I panic that the challenge of strength is starting now. I didn't mean now! Does he mean now?! Is he coming to smash me?!

"I NEED THREE DAYS!!!"

The hippie translates, "Three days to prepare!"

The troll returns to his squat and waves dismissively at us. I think I'm supposed to prepare in the cage. I cannot prepare in the cage. The hippie is way ahead of me, he says, "No, he must leave to prepare."

The troll says, "Why?" I actually understood some troll talking. !

"Because I need human food to make me strong. Troll food makes you weak."

The hippie translated. The troll stands up, indignant. I see his anger festering in him. I think I see bulges here and there. Many stories say that trolls get so angry they explode. Am I about to see a troll explode in anger? This could be awesome.

The hippie sputters an argument, "It's a challenge!"

The hippie is stupid because this calms the troll down. Now I have to go through three days of hell trying to figure out how to beat this troll and we almost had him right now. This whole nightmare for the whole city, dead dogs and backpackers, and children! It could all have been done right now. I keep replaying in my mind: the troll bursting, then us crawling out of this stupid cage, finally me being a town hero.

The hippie tells me that the troll curses my bloodline if I don't come back for the challenge. Most of my life I would have laughed at a blood curse. ...

The hippie says, "I'll see you in three days. My name is Paul." You bastard. You have to tell me your name, to guilt me, to make sure I know your life is resting on my shoulders and I have to return to save you. It's not enough that I'm blood cursed? Yes, two other lives, and really the fate of the whole city rests on me. Go #$%& yourself, Paul, you selfish bastard.

The troll takes me out of the cage. Paul says, "I challenge you too." I can't understand what the troll says, but I'm pretty sure he's not accepting multiple challenges.

I say, "You can't eat them until our challenge is complete. Their lives are tied to mine." Paul translates. The troll looks very irritated, very very irritated.

I walked out of there fast. Very, very fast. The clean air made me sneeze. I had been getting used to the troll stench. I realized now how queasy I was. Fear and adrenaline had kept it at bay, but passing out is bad for you. So's troll farts. I threw up my minimal stomach contents in a chunky patch of snow. But that's ok, because I was far enough from the cave now and I could run... kind of... broken ribs.

I was trying to figure out how I would explain things to Runa when I saw the oddest thing. Some colorful blob was coming toward me, like a carpet store on feet. I suppose it was just a bundle of shawls and blankets. Anyway, that patchwork quilt of a... person? Was really happy to see me.

It was Runa. That little chicken was coming to the troll's den to try to rescue me. And she was dressed up as an old woman... of color. Please don't think she's racist. 'K everybody is, but she sincerely believes trolls don't like to eat black people and she was sincerely afraid of being eaten. Trust me, racism is in every country and this isn't the weirdest version I've seen of it. Anyway.

I turned her around and we hurried home. I didn't need her guidance. I knew my way home from the troll bridge very well now. I started explaining the story to her. How I had to go back. How there were others, but we couldn't get them now. How I had to win a challenge of strength with a troll. Runa promised to make me something magic for my challenge. My heart soared with hope.

That was kind of a bad thing, because I kind of held off my planning until I saw what magic she gave me. A day passed. Two days passed. Did I mention that I have a blood curse to go back and face this troll and I have NO plan?! But Runa keeps me waiting. She has very good excuses. Like, you can't get real magic books at the public library. She stayed up all of the final night. I passed the night between rousing fits of anxiety and the sweating sleep you get from exhaustion. In the morning my sunken-eyed girlfriend presented me with a string. She said nothing could cut this string. It wasn't 100 yards. It wasn't even one yard. It was 2 inches. I wasn't going to be tying down a sleeping troll with this. ... !

I was desperate for my cheese stones. I hadn't even gotten cheese stones. I ran to the refrigerator. I whittled down cheese into smooth stones. They looked nothing like stones. I tried sticking in gravel. How stupid are trolls anyway? Will he just fall for anything? I was trying to think of how to play the cheese challenge, I was trying to think of a follow-up challenge (sometimes the hero has to do more than one trick) or just a better challenge. I was fantasizing about the town carrying me on their shoulders after beating the troll. I was high on my brilliance. High on brilliance I hadn't thought of yet. In other words, I was useless for thinking. I was trying to make sure I had everything I needed to go on my quest. I remembered Paul telling me his name, that selfish clown. I suddenly felt my heart being crushed as if by a hand. Paul's life. Some nun's life. The village children. Me. Why did I have to do this? I can't. It's not my choice; this invisible hand is about to stop my heart. I'll die if I try.

I wondered where my luggage was.

Don't blame me for being selfish. You never heard the greet grrreeet ggreett. You never had to walk back into a bubble of violence after you got safely out. If, if you're in a domestic bubble of violence, maybe you go back for a little brother or sister. Not a Paul. Why did he have to tell me his name? And that nameless church lady. They're not family. So many people died, little kids even. What's one or two more meals to the troll? Someone else will fix it. Someone stronger and smarter than me. Someone tougher who can handle that sound. Runa should fix it. It's her fucking fault for bringing Paul and everyone and ME into this! Why can't she fight her own demons!?

Blood curse. Blood curse. I was trying to think scientifically if trolls had the ability to curse people. They're not witches. They don't have religious power, I don't think. Seriously. How does a blood curse work? How does love work? How much are you supposed to sacrifice to... ? I miss Runa just from fantasizing about getting on the plane. This stress makes being lonely and catatonically depressed in the snow look fun.

There's a door. And on the other side of that door is anything. I can go anywhere. No guards are going to make me go to the cave. I can just go anywhere. ANYWHERE. Or I can walk a stu-

pid f'ing path that is the only path I know because of traumatically getting lost. The same
way. Repeatedly. I wanted to die anyway a little
while ago. Am I afraid of dying? No. Yes, but no.
The bubble of violence. That bone greet sound.
It's really, really YOU KNOW?! That smell. It's
so petty and childish when people's lives are
at stake, I know. I just don't ever want to smell
that smell again. Could you crawl through raw
sewage to save a stranger's life?

The door's open because I don't have an ex-
cuse to stand still anymore. Runa is sending me
off. Walk out the door. Start toward the cave.
You don't really have to go. The terrible thing
you're about to do, lying to Runa is the least of
it. Are you really going to leave people for dead?
Abandon a city? Leave love, that stupid, sense-
less bond of believing in each other? Maybe
you are.

You can turn off the path at any time. Any
time you want. Make the decision.

One pocket full of sweaty cheese balls. One
pocket with an "unbreakable" magic string so
small that it kept getting lost in my lint. A

Swiss Army knife. A cell phone. And tissue to blow my nose. Today's a troll killing day.

Now I'm standing with a machete, too fat-handled for me to get my hands around. In between, there was ALOT of walking. I think I got lost going to the only place I never get lost. There was alot of planning and practicing lines. There was alot of disappointment that the cheese stones started breaking up in my pocket before I could pretend to crush them. There was alot of me thinking that I would speak to the troll with a hero voice. But I couldn't find that voice and Paul still had to translate anyway. And for some reason instead of the troll cutting my unbreakable string first I was cutting the troll's rope belt, thicker than my wrist, much thicker than the blade on my Swiss Army knife. The troll had loaned me his belt knife, with a handle so thick that I could only hug it or sandwich grip it. And I don't know about you, but I can't much swing a hug.

I know people's lives are supposed to flash before their eyes. I didn't know if it was true. Remember, until recently I was a skeptic of everything. But for me it was different. People with normal lives maybe face death with visions of their life. My mind wasn't normal. My mind was a chaos sandwich. I went from sensory deprivation to sensory overload, nothingness to massive stress, constant strategizing, with new smells of incredible intensity, sounds of remarkable disturbance, sights not to be believed, too big, too (dammit, what would a writer say for something like fantastical, but way bigger than that word, because when "fantastical" is really real, then saying "fantastical" sounds stupid) too much. So my mind was in a vertigo of remembering sensory deprivation and feeling sensory overload. Imagine your nose was closed for months for, say surgery. And they finally took off the bandages and you breathed in troll fart. Flashbacks to my life would've been great. I could've flashed back to my childhood karate classes and thought about my lessons on how to ignore the pain and fatigue, and visualize my fist breaking through the board. When I taught in Japan I had a student who broke his hand breaking a brick for his black belt. Doesn't matter! At the time I didn't remember anything about karate. There was no idealism, there was only reality.

The machete was liftable, but heavy enough that I would wobble. I wouldn't be able to rest arms up and get a good swing down. Worst, my sandwich grip meant the knife would loosen immediately on impact, limiting the transfer of force. And now my damn palms were sweating!

Arms up.

Flicker. The belt disappeared for a moment.

Not now. I need to see this. I need this reality to be real so I can fix it. Don't not be real right now.

Flicker. Wait, nothing disappeared that time. Not the belt, not the troll. What the hell flickered? I flickered. Why did I flicker? Am I dying in the snow? Am I asleep in the gingerbread house? I'm in the au pair house, a hospital, America? I'm having a nightmare/hero dream. Just let me finish this dream. Don't wake up yet.

The sweat stings my eyes. This is not a dream.

I knew that I wouldn't be able to cleave that rope with one swing. I was afraid that Runa's magic string wasn't shit. I didn't believe in myself and I almost flickered myself out of existence. Have you ever almost flickered yourself out of existence? I had to believe in me. And I couldn't meditate myself to any other reality. I had to do the reality I was in. I had to cut this uncuttable rope. Or face a troll in man-to-man combat. I had his knife.

Arms down.

If I could just get a good wound on him... maybe immobilize him. I could go rescue the others. I could get their help to finish him off. No way I could wound his chest with that ungainly weapon and our height difference. Maybe I could chop off some toes, or stab his instep. But if I had the strength to chop off those toes, I could probably cut that rope too.

I began to spit on my palms. But I wasn't spitting on my hands for grip, not with all that sweat. I was putting on the show. I needed him to cower, look away, make some kind of mistake. I invoked gods and spirits. But Jesus doesn't come for non-believers. Neither does Odin or Buddha. I summoned the power of the skies. He looked nervous and superstitious, but he wasn't exactly scared. So I howled and stomped. I beat my chest. I scraped my feet on the ground like a bull. I tried to look savage, like a Maori or something. I almost moved to New Zealand instead of Norway. Focus! Maori! Savage! A life of warrior bravery!

The troll only looked on curiously. *Flicker.* But the dust was having an effect. He coughed a little. He blinked. He was too far away. I would have to run in to chop his toes. He would see me coming. I kicked dust more. And more and more. He coughed, he cringed. So did I, but it didn't matter. The breeze took the dust straight to him. He was engulfed! I brought up the giant rusted blade. Now was my chance. Run at his feet! Hack his toes! Maybe I could get his Achilles heel! Slash that artery in the leg. Where's that artery in the leg?!?

Or chop the rope. Or chop the rope. Or chop the rope.

Why would I chop the rope? Why wouldn't I attack straight to the beast? That rope will get me killed.

Flicker. Which way is that flicker for? Both ways? Doesn't matter. I want to attack his feet.

But...

Runa spent three days making magic for me.

No she didn't. Spent days trying to find an idea. She spent a night making magic she doesn't understand and never tested.

She spent a night making magic.

It doesn't matter. I have to live to use the magic. I can save it for a rainy day. It doesn't have to be now.

...

I screamed like a Viking. Welcome me to Valhalla!

HAAAAAAAAAAAAAAAAAAAGGGGGHHH!

I dug my fingernails into the rotten wood handle so my grip wouldn't slip. I bonded with the splinters. I tightened every sinew in my body especially around the cracked ribs. I closed my dirt-filled eyes and tore that rusted blade down from the sky onto...

the rope.

I only cut 80% through. It was the perfect cut like I rolled a crit and still it only went 80% through. The troll was still hacking and squinting. I quickly sawed a few strokes with the blade. It wasn't made serrated, but bad treatment gave it a rough edge. 90% through.

I screamed again and snuck in a little chop. I chopped a couple more. Was the rule only one chop? Didn't make sense to have a strength contest with unlimited chops, but if he caught me, I could play dumb. 95% through, but that last bit was smashed in the wood and harder to cut. I laughed with fake mania, maybe a little real mania. I ran forward and bit the rope looking sideways at my hideous friend, kicking back dirt. I laughed as loud as I could through my teeth. I felt the Swiss Army knife in my back pocket. Tiny scissors! I pulled it out. I fumbled with the tiny pull grooves. My hands were numb and unsteady from hyper-gripping the machete. I fumbled the whole knife out of my hands. Why now?! I dipped quick to pick it up. I dipped too shortly and I started standing before I really grasped it. WHY NOW!!?? I picked it up right, I snipped the last of the rope. I tossed the knife away and fell back laughing hysterically. The machete was beside me, not in my hands. But I couldn't fake a show of strength anyway. That burst of exertion had spent everything I had to give. I felt like all the blood was gone from me and I sucked at the air in between my hysteria like I was 3 thousand meters higher in altitude. Short quick breaths, though. Cracked ribs are terrible.

The troll stared at me crossly. The dust wasn't quite gone, but he didn't make the tiniest cough or blink. I'd made a mistake. When I was choosing to cut the rope before, I thought I would still have a chance to cut at his feet. I hadn't meant to spend everything I have. Every drop of stamina. I didn't know I wouldn't be able to stand. I didn't know that I shouldn't be able to lift the only weapon.

The troll stomped over in one appallingly easy stride. He picked up his knife. My laughing was gone now. I only wheezed at the air asthmatically. But I stared at him with the strongest eyes I could make. And I think my eyes were very strong just then. But I was sure that I would die.

But when he reached down again, he didn't grab my leg. He grabbed the cut rope. He examined it and huffed in disbelief. But then he only shrugged and laid it down again. He could cut through a rope too, if I could. A second wind filled me. I didn't quite jump to my feet, but

I did dart up to a straight sit. I shook my finger at him. I stood up. I nearly reeled off balance. I still didn't have my strength or head on me. But I awkwardly kicked his rope off the log. I pointed to myself authoritatively. I took the string out of my pocket. I held it as close to his stinking rotting carcass-breath as my puny arms could reach, and I laid it on the log, well centered and parallel. Then I opened my hands to it, his challenge.

He laughed. He laughed so hard that one of the pieces of... something... that was stuck on his teeth came flying off at me. I had to side-step it. But a bit of spit that flew with it hit me under the eye. I felt immediately infested with worms, but I wiped it off and just stared him down.

When he was done laughing, he prepared to chop our string. Runa's and mine. I couldn't help thinking about all those Hollywood movies. There's always some genius who develops a new technology or technique. And it always works the first try. And I'm not an engineer, but I'm sure every engineer who sees a Hollywood movie wants to tear somebody's ears off and explain to them slowly how it takes a team of guys developing something just the least bit novel and it still never works the first try.

The point is... *DID* Runa test this magic? At all? With dull scissors? With her teeth? I realize now I didn't. Maybe I was afraid to see it fail, or question Runa who stayed up all night. But I don't believe in magic. I believe in trolls. She made me believe everything. But I don't intrinsically believe in magic yet. I haven't had enough time. I haven't seen it yet. Do I have to believe in it for it to work? Magic and George Michael got to have faith.

The troll was done laughing. He leaned in close to the log to spot the string. He took a wider stance. He fixed a good grip on the knife. He raised his big muscly, jiggly arm up for a mighty drop. Apparently he wasn't going to fool about with a swing that matched the string. His head had to come up too, but he squinted hard to eyeball that tiny string. I thought he was trying to chop the log in two too, just to prove a point. He sneered and made some bass-speaker version of a hiss as his arm dropped.

The log shook, but didn't break twain. Splinters flew up. The troll leaned in and so did I, despising the dangle of his greasy hair coming near me, but too desperate to miss the results. The string lay, not only whole, but unshifted by the violence. He had missed. He grabbed the log and kept one hand near the string. He kneeled closer. He brought his arm back farther. Maybe if I distracted him, he would cut his own hand off. His yellow and bloodshot eyes flashed or something like it and with a disturbing gurgling huff he swung again. I wasn't ready, but I shouted a laugh mid-swing. He ignored it. He swung again. And again.

He missed and missed. He fumed. He cursed. Veins started to bulge on his forehead. He continued to swing, but the 2-inch string was too small for him, or the magic of it turned his blade away? He wasn't smart enough to just do a little cut and rely on his massive size. The vein on his forehead burst. Brown blood ran out. His forearms bulged. His chest swelled. He closed his eyes. He chopped his own hand after all. A finger fell to the other side of the log, but he didn't stop chopping. I was winning. I had tricked the troll.

And he froze. Maybe this is where he turns to stone. But only his limbs froze. His chest rose and dropped with gargantuan breaths. The swelling subsided. As his torso heaved, his head locked exactly on the knife before him on the log. The blade rested. In a deep notch of wood. And on each side of that notch, a bit of string was sticking up. He'd hit the string. Too soon. He hadn't exploded yet. He began to lift the blade. The blade was blocking my... our view of the string. The tips of the string came down to rest on the wood again. The knife had dulled with cleaving so much wood. Underneath that bent blade, the string...

... was whole.

The troll started swelling again. I realized I didn't know what kind of explosions trolls do. Was it just gross and bloody or was it danger-ous? Like a bomb? I realized I didn't want to get either.

I ran and dove behind a tree as a skunk spray of blood and a cloud of bone shrapnel burst in an ear-ringing blast of warbling air and seemingly undulating trees. I didn't know if every-thing was loud or everything was quiet, but as I staggered out from behind the tree I knew it was good I took cover. His bones' shards had sunk so deep in the wood, they clearly would have passed my flesh and maybe even punc-tured my own bone.

The troll was dead.

No more tolls to be paid.

I left Norway. With Runa. Runa was never a traveler before, but she became one. Wasn't hard to get me out of town. The locals treated me like a legend, but the nightmares never stopped until I left.

By the way, Aksel grew up and got a deaf girlfriend. He learned sign language for her and talked through that, and after he got used to speaking through signing, he even started oral talking again. I never heard his voice myself. He told me in letters, though.

But everywhere I went there were monsters. I don't know if Runa secretly researched places to move to that had bad faeries and evil spirits, or if we just always came across those things because she believes in EVERYTHING. I suppose it sounds cool to you. Like I'm a monster hunter. But I know one of these days I won't prevail. I'm going to die by something that you don't even believe in.

I don't know how to advise you. I wanna say, "If you can help it. Don't believe these things. It's the safest thing. Just set your mind and don't believe any of it at all." So many bad things in this world go away if you just choose not to believe in them. Just... then you can't fight them. And some people like Runa, and children, can't choose not to believe. So...